Gabe picked up a linen napkin and shook it open before placing it gently across her lap. Sophie froze as his hand brushed her thigh.

Even through the thin fabric of her scrubs she could feel his body heat, and the sensation tied her tongue in knots as she struggled to make conversation. But her brain seemed to have shut down for the day—which wasn't surprising, given the day she'd had, but it did leave her feeling at a distinct disadvantage.

His presence put knots in more places than just her tongue. Her stomach was doing so many somersaults she wasn't sure if she was going to be able to eat, despite the fact that she was starving. She didn't know what to think about Gabe yet, or about the reaction he provoked in her. She didn't want to be so aware of him. She wanted to be neutral. She wanted to be Switzerland. She didn't want to find him attractive but that was exactly what was happening. She didn't know what it was yet—his strength? His eyes? His solidness? He seemed dependable, and he gave her confidence in this unfamiliar environment.

But it was more than confidence. Having him nearby heightened her senses. And she realised then what it was.

He made her feel alive.

Dear Reader

This story has been floating around in my head for a while. Like so many of my ideas, it started to take shape when I got talking to a man who had just spent six months working in Antarctica. He told me some interesting tales about various accidents and emergencies that he'd encountered, and that got me thinking about what it would be like to move to the bottom of the world.

What type of people would choose to live and work in those extreme conditions? And what hardships would they face even in the twenty-first century?

I spent far too much time on research, but that gave me a very clear sense of the type of man Gabe Sullivan is. He loves a challenge, and is exactly the type of man I can imagine thriving in Antarctica—and he is the perfect man to melt Sophie's heart.

Sophie had to travel to the end of the earth to find love again—but isn't that something we would all be willing to do?

Enjoy!

Emily

A KISS TO MELT HER HEART

BY
EMILY FORBES

First published in Great Britain 2015
by Mills & Boon, an imprint of Harlequin (UK) Limited,
Eton House, 18-24 Paradise Road, Richmond, Surrey, TW9 1SR

© 2015 Emily Forbes

ISBN: 978-0-263-25802-8

Emily Forbes began her writing life as a partnership between two sisters who are both passionate bibliophiles. As a team, 'Emily' had ten books published. One of her proudest moments was winning the 2013 Australia Romantic Book of the Year Award for *Sydney Harbour Hospital: Bella's Wishlist*.

While Emily's love of writing remains as strong as ever, the demands of life with young families has recently made it difficult for them to work on stories together. But rather than give up her dream Emily now writes solo. The challenges may be different, but the reward of having a book published is still as sweet as ever.

Whether as a team or as an individual, Emily hopes to keep bringing stories to her readers. Her inspiration comes from everywhere, and stories she hears while travelling, at mothers' lunches, in the media and in her other career as a physiotherapist all get embellished with a large dose of imagination until they develop a life of their own.

If you would like to get in touch with Emily you can email her at emilyforbes@internode.on.net

Books by Emily Forbes

Tempted & Tamed!

A Doctor by Day...
Tamed by the Renegade

The Honourable Army Doc
Dare She Date the Celebrity Doc?
Breaking the Playboy's Rules
Sydney Harbour Hospital: Bella's Wishlist
Georgie's Big Greek Wedding?
Breaking Her No-Dates Rule
Navy Officer to Family Man
Dr Drop-Dead-Gorgeous
The Playboy Firefighter's Proposal

Visit the author profile page at
millsandboon.co.uk for more titles

FOR MY DAD
1935–2014
I MISS YOU

CHAPTER ONE

Hobart, Tasmania, February 26th

'ARE YOU SURE you want to do this?'

Sophie could see the concern in Luke's grey eyes and she appreciated it, but she'd made up her mind and she wasn't going change it now. She'd come too far. She *couldn't* stop now. And Luke should know that. They had been friends since they'd both been teenagers and there was only one person who knew Sophie better than Luke did—but Danny was gone now.

She squeezed his hand in what she hoped was a reassuring fashion, although she suspected she needed more reassurance than he did. His hand was warm in the chill of the hospital. Sophie didn't normally feel the cold. She had grown up in Tasmania, the wild but beautiful southern end of Australia, and cold weather was something she was used to, but the air felt frosty today. Maybe it was nervousness—not about the surgery, having her appendix out was a minor procedure—but her future plans were ambitious although she wasn't about to admit to any misgivings at this point.

She wrapped the towelling dressing gown around her body a little more firmly to ward off the chill as she said, 'I need to get away.'

'I understand that,' Luke replied, 'but why don't you take a holiday instead.'

Sophie looked at him. She wasn't in a vacation mood. 'What would I do on a holiday?' she asked.

'I don't know. Relax?'

'I don't need to relax and I don't want time to myself, I've got too much of that already. Holidays are meant to be shared with someone and we both know I have no one now. I don't want to go on a holiday but I do need to go some place where the memories won't follow me. Everywhere I look around here things remind me of Danny and I can see it in people's faces too. Every time they see me I remind them that Danny isn't here. I need to move on and I can't do that here. It's too hard. I need some space to get my head together.'

'I miss him too, Soph, but I'm not sure that spending a winter in Antarctica is necessarily the right place to get your head together.'

'It's not a whole winter, it's only seven weeks.'

'*If* the other doctor gets back. Otherwise you're there for winter. That's seven months.'

Seven months. Sophie knew that could seem like a lifetime. Danny had been dead for seven months. She knew exactly how long each day, each hour, each minute could seem.

But she also knew she couldn't stay in Hobart. She needed to get away and give her grief, and her guilt, time to fade. She knew she'd never forget, she didn't *want* to forget, but she did want to be able to live her life without memories of Danny shadowing her every move. She missed him but she missed her old self too. She wanted a chance to find the old Sophie, the one who had smiled and laughed, and she suspected it would be easier to remember how she used to be if she wasn't constantly being reminded of what she'd lost.

Her mind was made up and Luke should know that once she made up her mind she very rarely changed it. She tried to appease him. 'I appreciate your concern but it's not like I don't know what to expect.'

'Theory and practice are two very different things. I'm not pretending I understand the technicalities of your job but I do know about working in difficult environments and having to rely on others to get the job done. Working in Antarctica can't be the same as working in a city with all the support networks.'

'I know exactly what type of situations I might need to deal with,' she said. 'I admit I haven't worked in quite the same conditions but I have worked with the Antarctic Medicine Unit for two years. I have to trust everyone to do their part and they have to trust me to do mine.'

'But are you ready?'

Sophie knew what Luke was asking. It wasn't a question about her skills as a doctor, he'd have to trust her on that, it was a question about her state of mind. Sophie knew he was concerned about her and he deserved an honest answer.

'I don't know.' She'd been working towards this goal for the past six months—it had given her something to focus on since losing Danny. It had stopped her going crazy with grief and loneliness. It had seemed like a good idea but now that the moment was here, and sooner than she'd expected, she just had to hope she was making the right decision. 'I think I'm ready. The powers that be in the Antarctic programme seem to think so and I'm their best option. I *have* to be ready. They need me and I need to go.' She had to trust that the decision makers knew what they were doing. She knew her medical skills would be sufficient and she must have passed all the psych tests or they wouldn't be sending her. She had to believe she was ready.

This move would be a test for her. She knew that but she wanted to push herself, she *needed* to challenge herself. Danny had brought out the best in her, he had helped her to shine, and she was finding it hard to believe she'd be okay without him. That she *could* be okay. Danny had been her first and only love, and she'd never imagined having to live without him, but that was her reality. She needed to know if she could survive on her own.

She knew Luke was worried for her but she had to do this.

'I realise I'll either love it or hate it,' she continued, 'but I want to do something. I *have* to do something. I can't stay here and, to be honest, while I'll admit I'm nervous I'm also excited. I've been living day to day, getting up in the morning just aiming to get through one more day. This goal has given me something to look forward to. It's given me a reason to keep going.'

She knew that if the psychologists heard her last sentence they'd probably think twice about sending her to the ice. She didn't want Luke to think she was a basket case too so she tried to explain her feelings more succinctly.

'I get up in the morning and the house is quiet. There's none of Danny's stuff lying around, getting in my way. There are no piles of shoes, different ones for hiking, running, riding, paddling, abseiling and gardening. No ropes or tents or backpacks to trip over. No maps spread across the kitchen table.

'I'm never going to get that back and I miss it. I miss him. I miss listening to his big plans, listening to him plan our future and the future of the business. I felt like he took my future with him and this might be my chance to get it back. It won't be the same future, I've lost that, but perhaps it could be worth something.'

'Why haven't you told me this before? I thought you were coping.'

'I *am* coping.' She was, most days. 'But that's all I'm doing. I'm not living and I want to live again. I've lost Danny but I've also lost myself. I don't want to be sad and lonely any more. I need to get moving. I have to do *something*. This might make or break me but I have to try it.' She smiled. 'You can't pretend you're not a little bit jealous. I know this type of adventure would be right up your alley.'

Luke laughed. 'You're right. It's exactly the sort of thing I'd love to have a crack at. Danny would have too.' He paused and considered her carefully before continuing. 'Are you sure you're doing this for you and not out of some misguided tribute to Danny?'

Sophie knew that Danny was part of the reason she was going. Despite working for the Antarctic Medicine Unit for two years she hadn't ever originally intended to leave the mainland and head three thousand plus kilometres south to Antarctica. She and Danny and Luke had been inseparable since high school but the boys had been the adrenalin junkies while she had been far more conservative. Maybe this adventure was out of character for her but she wasn't foolish enough to venture out of her comfort zone without careful consideration of her reasons.

She thought Danny would be proud of her but that wasn't her main motivation. She had been going quietly mad, sitting in Hobart. There were too many memories. She hoped this adventure would be the catalyst to allow her to start again. To begin the next chapter of her life. A life without Danny.

'I think he would be proud of me for doing this,' she admitted, 'but I'm not crazy enough to take up this challenge without believing I can handle it.'

'You know I promised Danny that if anything ever happened to him I'd look after you?' Luke said.

Sophie frowned. 'You did?'

'Of course. We had to consider the possibility of things going wrong on one of our treks. We had to do risk-management assessments for every expedition and we discussed what we'd do in the worst-case situation. We had to hope for the best but prepare for the worst. Neither of us ever expected that something would happen that wasn't related to work but either way the result is the same. We planned for this and discussed it, always hoping we wouldn't need to worry about it for many years, but a promise is a promise, no matter when it's needed.'

Danny and Luke ran an adventure holiday company, catering to all the adrenalin junkies who travelled to Tasmania to explore the wilderness. Had run, she should say. The business was now Luke's. He'd bought Danny's share from her, but he was right. Every time Danny had gone off on a trek she had lived in fear of a phone call telling her something had gone wrong, but she'd never anticipated the phone call would come when he was just out for a weekend ride on the outskirts of Hobart. Danny had spent most of his days in the wilderness, living on the edge—she hadn't expected his days to come to an end in the city.

Getting knocked off his bike had been a stupid way for someone who'd spent his life trekking and white-water rafting and abseiling down cliff faces to die. He had simply gone off for a ride one morning. He'd kissed her goodbye as she'd left for work, and she hadn't seen him alive again. The driver of the car that had killed him had been overtaking a truck on a blind corner. He'd smacked head on into

Danny and the impact had been so severe that he hadn't survived the head and chest injuries he had sustained.

And just last week Sophie had learned that the driver of the car had been released from jail. He had served six months for taking Danny's life. It made her feel sick, just thinking about the unfairness of it all.

She was glad she was leaving. She couldn't imagine how she would feel if she ever came face to face with the man responsible for her husband's death. If she met him in the street she didn't think she could be held responsible for her actions. She didn't care that he'd expressed remorse. His stupidity had cost Danny his life. She knew she should try to forgive him but she hadn't been able to yet. She didn't know if she'd ever be able to.

She knew her anger at the driver was magnified by her own guilt. If she hadn't taken an extra shift that day, Danny wouldn't have been out riding. He would have been home with her.

She should have been with him. If she had been he wouldn't be dead. But guilt wasn't going to bring him back. She needed to move past that but it was difficult when everywhere she looked she saw Danny. They'd been tied together their whole lives and it was hard to move on when so many things reminded her of shared times. She knew she had to get away. That was the only way she was ever going to recover. It was the only way she was going to get over her guilt.

'I don't feel right about saying goodbye without at least checking your frame of mind,' Luke continued.

'That's why I'm doing this,' Sophie explained. 'I'm tired of people asking me how I am or, worse, saying nothing because they don't know what to say. When Danny was killed my dreams died with him. It's time for me to make some new dreams.'

For as long as she could remember she had always made three-year plans but the plans she'd made with Danny had come crashing down seven months ago and now she was a thirty-one-year-old widow. She needed a new plan.

'I feel as though I should be trying harder to stop you,' Luke said, 'but I get the impression you're not going to listen to me.'

Sophie smiled. 'You're right, but that doesn't mean I don't appreciate your concern.'

'If you can look me in the eye and promise me you know what you're doing, I'll feel like I've kept my side of the bargain with Dan.'

'I'll be fine and I like to think Danny would be proud of me.'

Luke leaned over and kissed her cheek. 'You're right, he would be proud of you, I'm proud of you too. Just make sure you don't do anything that makes me sorry I didn't try harder to talk you out of this.'

'Dr Thompson?' Their conversation was interrupted by one of the nursing staff. 'We're ready for you now.'

Sophie stood and hugged Luke. 'It'll be fine. *I'll* be fine. I promise,' she said, before she followed the nurse off to Theatre.

CHAPTER TWO

Date: March 7th
Temperature: -7°C
Hours of sunlight: 13.9

THE SEAT BELT WAS pressing into Sophie's still-tender abdomen and it was starting to irritate her now. Having had her appendix removed just a few days before her adventure wasn't ideal but she'd had no other option.

She was determined to be on this plane and she hadn't been about to let something as relatively minor as prophylactic surgery stop her. Any Australian doctor who wanted to work at one of the Antarctic stations had to have their appendix removed before they could be sent south. This clause didn't apply to anyone else—the doctor would be able to remove anyone else's troublesome appendix on the ice but the Australian Antarctic Programme didn't want to risk the station doctor. The surgery was non-negotiable but in Sophie's mind it was a relatively minor procedure and certainly something she had been happy to agree to. But she hadn't expected the tenderness to last for so many days.

She undid her belt and stood up. She could stretch her legs and her abdominals at the same time. She wandered to the cockpit, seeking company. She was the sole passenger from Hobart to the Antarctic airfield. The plane would return filled with summer expeditioners heading home for the winter but on this leg she had the entire cabin to herself.

She'd spent most of the four-and-a-half-hour flight reading the numerous documents she'd been given, trying to work out which ones were the most important. Her trip had been fast-tracked and she knew she hadn't had the same time to prepare as most others would have had. But she was tired of reading and it couldn't be too much longer before they landed. It had been dark when they'd left Hobart but the sunrise had followed them as they'd flown west, eventually catching up with them, and Sophie had watched as the sky had turned pink and lightened as they'd flown over the ocean.

She knocked on the cockpit door, eager to check with the flight crew what their ETA was. She felt like a kid on a long car trip. *'How much longer?'* She wanted to get the three-thousand-four-hundred-kilometre flight over and done with. She wanted to get to the ice.

'Perfect timing,' the pilot, said as he called her in. 'Have a seat. We've just started spotting the first icebergs.'

Sophie took a seat behind the captain and co-pilot and peered through the cockpit windows. The sea was calm and flat, a pond of dark blue dotted with white. The icebergs were stunning, crisp, pure and brilliant and all different shapes and sizes. But the ice was not pure white, like she'd expected, but lit with myriad shades of blue—turquoise, aqua, a hint of cerulean and the palest sky blue.

It was a serene, perfect vista and Sophie was mesmerised. She could hardly believe she'd done it. What at times had seemed almost impossible was now only incredible. She was almost in Antarctica.

'We should be landing in about thirty minutes.' The captain interrupted her daydreaming. 'The weather conditions look good, it should be a straightforward approach, but you should change into your survival clothing now. It will probably take you a while.'

Sophie had collected her red kitbag just prior to boarding the plane in Hobart. It contained the multiple layers she needed to wear to keep warm in the polar conditions. She'd had a brief lesson in getting dressed the previous day and she just hoped she remembered the order.

She returned to the cabin, pulled the bag out of the overhead locker and dumped the contents on her seat. She could feel the plane start its descent as she stripped off her shoes, sweatpants and jumper and pulled on thermal underwear before replacing the other layers. She stepped into her red waterproof pants, which were insulated with a down filling, making them rather cumbersome. She stuffed her shoes into the kitbag and then sat down to wrestle with the bulky insulated snow boots complete with thick rubber soles. She had some difficulty getting her feet into the boots—the puffy pants made bending awkward—but eventually she was able to lace up the white boots, which had the rather odd nickname of 'bunny boots'. She slipped her arms into the padded jacket and tugged a neck warmer over her head but decided the beanie and gloves could wait. She gathered her hair in one hand and tucked it inside her jacket, where it hung down between her shoulder blades.

By the time she'd finished and returned to her seat she could see through the window that the vast expanse of ocean was giving way to an equally vast expanse of ice and snow in the distance. She searched the horizon for signs of life, for buildings or communication towers, something, anything, to indicate that the icy plateau was inhabited. She could see miles and miles of ice, snow and ocean and eventually a few small buildings, which looked no bigger than shipping containers cobbled together, came into view. That would be the airstrip.

She knew not to expect to see a traditional tarred runway but she was nervous. She could see nothing that remotely resembled a landing strip. She knew from the mandatory flight briefing she'd had the previous day that the plane would land on a specially built pack-ice runway three kilometres long, but that didn't appease her nerves at all. She couldn't fathom how something as big and heavy as this plane could land safely on a runway made of ice. The flight briefing had covered information on the flight and the runway, as well as several topics on safety and survival in the Antarctic, but that didn't stop her from imagining the plane skidding out of control off the edge of the slippery landing strip.

She decided ignorance was bliss and turned away from the window, choosing not to watch as the plane approached the runway. She zipped up her jacket and dug her sunglasses out of her bag.

Standing at the top of the stairs, with the landing safely completed, the chill of the Antarctic autumn day took her by surprise. It was only minus seven degrees Celsius and the sun was shining, but the briskness of the wind on her face after the relative warmth of the plane was unexpected. She tugged her neck warmer up to cover the bottom half of her face and considered donning her beanie but opted just to pull the hood of her jacket over her head before she slipped her sunglasses over her eyes and made her way down the aircraft stairs.

In contrast to the relative silence on the plane, the airstrip was a hive of activity. She couldn't remember who she was supposed to look for and even if she could she doubted she'd find them. Everyone looked identical. They were all bundled up in matching government-issue red jackets, balaclavas or face masks and sunglasses as they went about their duties, making it impossible to recognise anyone.

The fluttering in her stomach, which she'd convinced herself was excitement, suddenly intensified as anticipation gave way to nervousness. Was she going to be able to handle this? All of a sudden living and working in this extraordinary environment with a group of strangers didn't seem quite so exotic and exhilarating.

But she remembered her promise to Luke and straightened her shoulders. She could do this. She *would* do it. And she'd return home stronger and surer and ready to get on with her life.

'Doc?' A thick-set man had separated himself from the bustle and was waiting for her at the bottom of the stairs. He stuck out a hand and Sophie shook it, rather awkwardly due to the thick gloves they both wore, as she took in what little she could see of him.

He was a few inches taller than her and wasn't wearing any head protection—no hat, no balaclava—just sunglasses. He was a big man but appeared to be muscular rather than fat and had hair that hung to his shoulders in thick blond ringlets. His nose was slightly hooked and his jaw was covered in a scruffy blond beard. His eyes were hidden but a cheeky smile lit up his face.

'I'm Alex, the FTO.'

From her previous dealings and background reading Sophie already thought of Antarctica as the land of acronyms but she was struggling to keep track of them all and couldn't remember what this one meant. She looked blankly at him until he qualified it for her.

'The field training officer.'

'Oh, right. It's nice to meet you.'

'I'll be driving you back to Carey Station but you've

got some time to kill first. I have to get the cargo squared away to take back with us.'

Sophie was surprised by Alex's strong Australian accent—a Queensland twang, she thought—and she realised she had expected to hear foreign accents, the kind of thing that happened when you travelled to the ski fields and the lift operators and ski instructors had European accents, even though the ski fields were in Australia. She'd been fooled by the surroundings into thinking she was in a foreign land—and she was—but this part of it was being run by Australians. It was obviously going to take her some time to adjust and she had another nervous moment as she realised that it was very likely that *nothing* would be as she'd expected.

'What do I need to do with my bags?' she asked, as she saw them being unloaded from the cargo hold. She'd been allowed three bags with a combined weight of fifty-five kilograms and, having no real concept of what she might actually need but knowing it would be impossible to get anything she'd forgotten, she'd used every ounce of her allowance. In addition to her own luggage she'd also been given the survival kit, which she had hauled down the airplane steps along with her carry-on luggage. Even though she was now wearing most of the contents of the bag, it was still bulky and she hadn't thought about the logistics of getting all her bags from the plane across the ice and snow to the buildings and to her transport. She had no idea what the procedure was.

'Is that them?' Alex pointed at her cases. Sophie nodded. 'Just the three?' She nodded again. 'I'll take care of it,' he offered. 'Give me your survival bag as well. I'll stow them in the Hägglund and I'll meet you inside the terminal when I'm done.'

Sophie didn't argue as Alex took her survival kit and

grabbed the first of her cases. She was relieved not to have to cart her heavy bags while negotiating the icy conditions.

She could see the over-snow vehicle parked a few metres from the plane. The Hägglund was an odd-looking machine and it reminded her of a childish drawing of a car crossed with a mini-tank. It looked like a box with windows set atop caterpillar treads, which Sophie knew would enable it to traverse the ice. Both the cabin and its attached trailer were square and boxy and painted bright red. Alex hoisted her bags into the attached trailer while Sophie headed for the building that he had indicated. It was difficult to walk in the cumbersome clothing, especially the heavily insulated bunny boots, and her progress felt slow and awkward.

When she finally reached the 'terminal' it turned out to be a rather makeshift building constructed out of several shipping containers, just as it had looked from the air, with a few minor modifications along the lines of some windows and a couple of doors. It also reminded her of a child's drawing and it lent a surreal air to her surroundings.

Inside, the building was full of people who, she assumed, were summer expeditioners. They were milling around, waiting to get on the plane that would fly them home for winter, but despite the crowd it wasn't any warmer inside the building. The only difference in here was that more people had their heads and faces uncovered.

'Dr Thompson?'

She turned at the sound of her name and, recognising the Scottish burr of the man's voice, she smiled as she greeted him. 'You must be John.' His accent was much more similar to what she'd expected to encounter. John was the doctor she had come to replace and while she had dealt with him before through the AMU, the Antarctic

Medicine Unit, it had only been over the phone, never in person, and it was good to be able to put a face to his name.

He was able to give her a brief handover but Sophie was relieved to hear he'd left detailed instructions for her at the station. Knowing he had more pressing things on his mind—his daughter's scheduled surgery—she insisted she would be fine. 'Just make sure you call with an update on Marianna's condition,' she said, before saying farewell to him as he made his way to the refuelled aircraft.

Alex appeared at her side as the terminal emptied of people. 'We're good to go,' he told her.

He kept up a steady stream of conversation from the moment she climbed into the Hägglund and she was grateful that he didn't appear to expect too much in the way of replies from her.

He was entertaining company, keeping her amused with stories from the ice and telling her what to expect. She was quite interested in how a rugby player from the warm climate of Queensland had adjusted to the indoor life at an Antarctic station.

'We spend more time outside than you'd think,' he responded. 'The weather is cold but it's often clear and fine. You'll be able to get out and go exploring. Do you know how to ride a quad bike?'

'No.' Sophie shook her head.

'No worries. I'll teach you. That's part of my role as the FTO. It's my job to train the other expeditioners, including you, in station safety procedures, survival skills, how to operate snowmobiles, quad bikes and the like. I'm also one of your medical support team.'

Sophie knew that some of the expeditioners had done some basic medical training and were able to assist her in an emergency situation, helping with suturing, anaesthetic monitoring and acting as scrub nurses among other things, but as Alex talked she found herself becoming increasingly nervous as it really sank in that she would be the only doctor for hundreds of miles and solely responsible for all the crew at the station.

She was feeling quite overwhelmed. She'd thought she'd be excited but everything was far more foreign than she'd anticipated, including the landscape. The pictures and videos she'd seen hadn't prepared her for the rather alien scenery that filled the windows. Vast expanses of ice stretched into the distance. She could see mountains of ice but the only thing that broke the expanse of white was the occasional rocky outcrop.

The landscape looked relatively flat but she could feel corrugations under the caterpillar treads of the Hägglund, making it seem as though they were going up and down over crests of waves. Alex told her that was exactly what happened. The wind formed the snow into drifts that then froze, making waves in the surface. In some places, where the ice rose up in thicker drifts that absorbed red light from the spectrum, the ice appeared more blue than white, but mostly it was a blinding glare that made her feel she needed to close her eyes even with her sunglasses on.

'Doc? We're almost here.'

Alex woke her as they approached the station. She hadn't meant to fall asleep but the interior of the over-snow vehicle was warm and cosy, and despite the excitement of her new surroundings she was exhausted. She hadn't slept the night before—she'd had to be at the airport by three-thirty in the morning and she hadn't seen much point in going to bed first so she'd stayed up, double-checking her packing. She'd taken out clothes and put in a few non-essential luxury items that other women who had worked on the ice suggested she take—a nice dress, decent shampoo, a thick bath towel, sheepskin boots—and as much as she hadn't wanted to miss anything on the seventy-kilometre trip from the airstrip to the station she'd been lulled to sleep by the monotonous sound of the diesel engine and the warmth of the cabin.

'I thought you might like a first glimpse of your temporary home,' Alex said, as they came over a crest in the snow.

The station was spread out before her. It was perched on the edge of a natural harbour and while Sophie had seen photos the scale still took her by surprise. Close to a dozen brightly painted buildings were scattered over the snow, as if someone had spilt a handful of children's building blocks. The buildings were a collection of shipping containers welded together to form larger structures, exactly the same as the buildings at the airstrip but on a bigger scale.

Sophie knew the bright paint scheme—red, yellow, blue and orange—was to make the buildings distinguishable from each other in blizzard conditions. The colour each 'shed' was painted depended on its function, but the brightness of the paint made the buildings look out of place, a blight on the landscape and a stark contrast to the ancient, icy plateau surrounding her.

A large dock poked out into the harbour and parked on the dock and scattered between the buildings were dozens of vehicles—trucks, graders, snowmobiles and trailers. Antennae and tanks, for water and gas storage, she suspected, sprouted out of the ground between the sheds, competing for space on the ice.

Her nervousness kicked up another notch. This was the station, her home for the next few weeks, and the little outpost of civilisation looked even more alien than the landscape.

'Welcome to Carey,' Alex said, as he brought the Häg-glund to a stop in front of the largest of the buildings. This building was painted bright red and it was one thing Sophie did recognise. It was called, not surprisingly, 'the red shed', and it housed the accommodation block, the kitchen and the medical centre, and it was where she expected to spend most of her time.

Sophie pulled her gloves back on, squared her shoulders and climbed out of the cabin as she told herself everything would all be all right.

The wind whipped past her cheeks, making them ache with the cold after the warmth of the vehicle. She reached for the neck warmer and pulled it up over the lower half of her face.

'Doc, welcome.'

A tall, solidly built man greeted her as he strode across the ground without a hint of the clumsiness she herself had felt as she'd negotiated the icy conditions. This man looked completely comfortable in the alien environment. He was dressed in a bright red cold-weather suit, identical to hers, but like Alex he had his head and face uncovered and exposed to the elements. The only concession he made to the conditions was in the form of sunglasses to protect against the blinding glare of the sun. Didn't anyone else think it was cold?

He stopped in front of her and Sophie looked up, way up.

He was several inches taller than her and she stood five feet seven inches. His dark hair was cropped short and sprinkled with a little salt and pepper, and a dark, neatly trimmed beard covered the bottom half of his oval-shaped face.

'I'm Gabe Sullivan, the station leader.'

So this was the man whose job it was to run Carey Station. This was her new boss.

He took his sunglasses off and extended his hand. His eyes were a dark chocolate-brown, kind and warming, and when he smiled at her, showcasing perfect white teeth framed by the darkness of his beard, Sophie forgot about being cold. Whereas Alex looked like a weekend surfer, Gabe Sullivan looked like a pioneer. Dark, rugged and strong. He looked like an explorer who was perfectly suited to this environment. He looked confident, like a man who could easily withstand the harsh elements of this climate, and as Sophie shook his outstretched, gloved hand she felt her nervousness recede as his gaze instilled confidence in her too.

Holding Gabe's hand and looking into his dark-eyed gaze, she had an immediate sense that things would be okay. It was a bizarre feeling to get from a complete stranger, it was a ridiculous notion, but she saw something in his eyes, felt something in the strength of his grasp, that made her feel as though she had made the right decision. That this adventure would not be a huge mistake.

She could sense the strength in him and she could draw her own strength from that. In the same way that Danny had made her a stronger person she felt the same sense of security and confidence when she looked at Gabe. Standing here, looking up at him, she knew she'd be all right. She could do this. She was ready for the next stage of her life.

Alex had opened the back of the Hägglund and was removing her luggage from the trailer. Sophie forced herself to remove her hand from Gabe's glove and break eye contact as she went to help with her bags. But Gabe was there before her.

'We'll get those for you,' he offered.

'I can manage,' she said, even though she wasn't certain

that she could. Her bags were heavy and her stomach muscles complained every time she moved too quickly, let alone tried to lift something heavy.

'Alex and I will do it,' Gabe insisted. 'You'll have plenty of opportunity to help out once you get used to moving in your cold-weather gear.'

Sophie wondered if he was normally this chivalrous or whether he knew she'd recently undergone surgery but, either way, she didn't bother arguing any further. It was nice to have someone look after her for a change so rather than debating the issue she graciously accepted his offer.

She did feel awkward in the padded overclothes and she suspected it would take some time for the bulky layers to feel comfortable. But even though her movement and her vision were restricted, she was grateful for the modern comforts. She couldn't imagine surviving out here without this clothing. She was no intrepid explorer. She wasn't really any sort of explorer. While Danny would have survived and thrived in these conditions, much like she suspected Gabe did, she knew she would be quite happy to experience the wilderness provided she had some twenty-first-century comforts.

Gabe and Alex retrieved her bags from the vehicle and Sophie followed them up the metal stairs to the red shed. She needed to steady herself with one hand on the rail of the steps, which were slick with a coating of ice, and she was glad she wasn't trying to wrestle with her bags at the same time.

The two-storey building towered above her as Gabe stomped his feet on the steel grid at the top of the stairs to dislodge any snow and Sophie followed suit. Alex deposited Sophie's bags beside her and excused himself, explaining he needed to return the Hägglund to the vehicle shed.

Gabe pushed open the door. It looked heavy and exactly

like a door one would find on a freezer room. As she stepped through it she could see that was precisely what it was. As Gabe closed the door softly behind her, she noticed an immediate increase in temperature for, despite the sunshine, the outside temperature remained well below freezing. She understood the point of the freezer door now—it wasn't to keep the cold in but to keep the cold out.

She found herself in what looked like a large mud room, similar to the drying rooms she'd seen in ski lodges. Around the edge of the room were open-fronted lockers with hanging space and shelving. Gabe directed her to one with 'Doc' written above it. 'You can keep your outer layer of clothes here—boots, jackets, pants, gloves.' His voice was deep and sounded like it held a smile, Sophie felt as if she could listen to him for hours. 'The shed is heated to around twenty degrees Celsius,' he continued, 'so you don't need much more than a layer of normal clothing once you're inside. If your clothes are damp or wet, make sure you hang them with some space between them so they dry effectively. Take your linings out of your boots if they are wet. If your socks are dry leave them on, otherwise change them.'

Sophie nodded and looked around, taking in the surroundings, as Gabe brought her bags into the room and then began to strip off his outer layers of clothing. Sophie hesitated before following. She wasn't sure exactly how many layers she was supposed to discard. He had mentioned normal clothing but stripping down to one layer would leave her standing there in her thermal underwear. She didn't think that was what he'd meant.

She looked to Gabe for guidance. His waterproof jacket was hanging on a peg above his boots. His waterproof pants came off next, followed by a fleecy pullover and his long-sleeved shirt. Sophie wondered how many more layers he was going to remove until she realised he had finished and was now standing, waiting for her, dressed in a simple black T-shirt and a pair of jeans.

She could see now that her first impression of him being solidly built had been correct. It was impossible to judge people's sizes accurately when they were encased in their cold-weather gear but now that he was standing in front of her in civvies she didn't have to imagine what he looked like. His shoulders were broad, his chest was muscular and his stomach was flat. His jeans hugged his thighs, showing off his long, lean legs. He was an impressive-looking man.

Realising it was probably inappropriate to be taking stock of him like this she averted her eyes and continued removing layers until she was clothed in her sweatpants and T-shirt. She was still wearing her thermals but she wasn't about to remove another layer and stand before Gabe in her underwear. She wasn't that confident and, if the truth be told, undressing at all in front of him was making her feel a little nervous. She'd taken off enough clothing for now, she just hoped it wasn't going to be much hotter inside the shed proper. She might regret her modesty.

Once she'd finished discarding clothing, Gabe opened the next door that led further into the red shed. 'Can you hold this for me?' he asked.

His voice was deep and smooth and matched his physique. He exuded a sense of calm while looking like a man who was used to being in charge, used to being listened to, used to having people follow his instructions. She supposed that was appropriate, given that he was in charge of the station, but Sophie got the sense that he wasn't a man you wanted to disappoint.

She held the door as Gabe picked up one of her bags and slung it over his shoulder, before grabbing the two remaining bags and leading the way out of the drying room.

'Let me take one of those,' Sophie protested. All she had to carry was her virtually empty kitbag.

'I've got it,' he replied. 'I know you've only just had your appendix out. I don't want to jeopardise your recovery by letting you lift and carry things you don't need to. You're far too important on this station to put you at risk.'

Sophie didn't argue any further. Gabe was twice her size. He had removed his shoes but he was still an inch or two over six feet tall and much heavier than she was. If he was going to insist on lugging her gear, she was happy to let him. She was willing to admit relief at not having to cart her suitcases.

She didn't ask how Gabe knew about her recent surgery. As Station Leader, he would have his finger on every pulse. She knew that the Human Resources department in Hobart would have prepared a file on her and that Gabe would have read it. The file would detail everything he might need to know, from her qualifications to the results of her psych tests to her next of kin. He would know how many years' experience she had as a doctor and that she was widowed. He would have read all the reports but he didn't mention any other personal details.

She was grateful for his help and his discretion. She followed him out of the drying room into a passageway. He didn't seem bothered by the fact that he was carting over fifty kilograms of her baggage. He didn't appear to be under any strain at all. His long-legged stride ate up the corridor and Sophie had to hurry to keep up with him.

'You've missed lunch but the cook will rustle something up for you as I'm sure you're hungry, and then I'll give you a tour of the station,' Gabe said over his shoulder. 'Unless you need to rest, in which case I'll show you straight to your room.'

The aroma of freshly baked bread wafted along the

corridor, teasing her taste buds. 'Something to eat sounds good,' she said, surprising herself. She had lost her appetite since Danny's death and she couldn't remember the last time she'd actually felt like eating. But suddenly she was starving.

Gabe turned and pushed open a door. He backed into a room and when Sophie followed she found herself in the mess hall. The kitchen equipment ran along the back wall to her left. Massive serving stations filled the centre of the room and several long communal tables were arranged between the serving area and the far wall. Sophie's eyes were drawn to a series of enormous windows on the far wall and she forgot all about the smell of freshly baked bread. She forgot she was in the kitchen. She forgot Gabe had brought her here to eat. She forgot she was hungry.

The view through the windows drew her across the room. The windows looked out over the icy plateau and across the blue waters of Vincennes Bay, and she couldn't resist a closer look at the harbour. She'd only caught a quick glimpse of the station's landscape as Alex had delivered her to the red shed and she was drawn to the contrasting colours of the buildings, the ice and the water. The views were glorious.

Half a dozen armchairs with plump cushions were positioned in front of the windows and she could just imagine curling up in one and staring out across the ice. It would be a constantly changing landscape, depending on the weather conditions, and more than likely would be enough to keep her occupied for hours.

'It's incredible, isn't it?' Gabe stood beside her.

She nodded and spoke in a whisper that seemed to fit the majesty of the view. 'I can't believe I'm going to live here for the next few weeks. At the end of the earth.'

Gabe was smiling at her. 'Just wait until you see Mother

Nature in all her glory. It's beautiful today when the sun is shining but if there's a blizzard it will seem as though someone has pulled a snow curtain over the windows. Every day is different and at times the weather can, and does, change in a matter of seconds. It's a beautiful but inhospitable landscape and, while you're welcome to explore it, it's imperative we make sure you're equipped to deal with it. I'll organise for Alex to give you some survival training as we can't let you out there until we're sure you're ready, but right now I think the first order of business is getting you fed.'

Gabe introduced her to Dom, the station chef, who served her a bowl of minestrone with freshly baked rolls still warm from the oven. Sophie's stomach rumbled as she quickly gathered her brown, shoulder-length curls into one hand, pulling them into a ponytail before securing it with an elastic band that was around her wrist. She flicked her hair back over her shoulder, picked up her spoon and dipped it into the soup. She bent her head and tasted it.

'Mmm, this is fabulous, thanks, Dom. I think I'll make you my first friend.'

She lifted her head and beamed at Dom and Gabe was stunned at the way her smile lit up her face and changed her from an attractive woman into a beautiful one. How did he get her to smile like that at him? He'd been mesmerised, watching her tie her dark curls back into a ponytail—he had always loved how women could so deftly change their hairstyles—but watching her play with her hair couldn't compare to watching her face light up with a full smile. She had two dimples, one in each cheek, and the sudden flash of the matching pair completely blindsided him. She was a gorgeous woman even if, in his opinion, she was too thin. Seeing her tuck into Dom's soup was a relief.

He knew that Sophie's husband had been tragically

killed only a few months ago and he'd had reservations about the Australian Antarctic Programme sending her down here so soon after the accident, but he'd been told that she'd passed all the tests and that they didn't have any other options. She was the best choice, they'd said, and he just had to hope it worked out. The only trouble was that if things didn't go according to plan, she became his problem, not the AAP's. He was the one in charge down here. He was the one left to sort out any mess. But seeing her eat relieved some of his apprehension. That was one less thing to worry about. Maybe she was naturally thin or maybe she'd lost weight after her husband had died, but at least she was eating.

To distract himself from thoughts of her dimples, he transferred her bags to her room while she ate, before returning to help settle her into the station. Their first stop on the way to her room was the storeroom.

'This is our version of a supermarket, and you can help yourself to anything in here that you need,' he told her as he waited for her to select linen, toiletries and other essentials from the shelves. 'This floor of the shed is primarily living and rec space. We have a gym, a climbing wall, an activity centre, a library, lounge and a cinema, so there's plenty to keep you occupied for any downtime. Everything of importance as far as your role is concerned is housed in the red shed. The other sheds are for stores, machinery, that sort of thing, although there is an area set up in one shed for those who like painting or woodwork or photography, etcetera. I'll show you that another time. The medical centre and your room are down this way.

'This is your donga,' he said as he pushed open yet another door, this one leading into a bedroom. 'And the medical centre is across the corridor.'

Sophie followed Gabe into her room. It was far from

spacious. Her bags were taking up most of the free floor space, leaving just enough room for the two of them to stand side by side. The air in the room felt charged and she had a sense of anticipation but she tried to tell herself it was just the circumstances, the excitement of her new surroundings, and had nothing to do with the man standing next to her. But she was aware of how much space he took up, and as there was no room for her to move she stood beside him as she checked out her quarters.

As small as it was, it contained all the essentials. There was a single bed with built-in furniture—a tiny desk, a wardrobe and plenty of shelves and under-bed drawers for storage. It reminded her of boarding school.

'I know it's pretty basic but this is actually one of the dongas that has been recently refurbished. And we don't want to make it too comfortable because we want people to get out of their rooms and socialise—it's important in this isolated environment—but we realise people do need some privacy. You'll have internet access for emails, et-cetera, but no video calls. The password and log-in details are here on your notice-board,' he said, as he pointed out a scrap of paper pinned to a board above the desk. 'All the dongas have single beds. That's not to say there aren't South Pole romances, we're not trying to deliberately make things difficult, but space is at a premium.'

'I don't think a single bed will bother me,' she said, knowing it was of little consequence to her.

'My room is next to yours. I also want to be close to the action but most of the accommodation is on the upper level. Now that most of the summer staff has left, I can arrange to move you upstairs if you'd prefer.'

'No.' Sophie shook her head. 'It makes sense for me to be close to the medical facilities.' She was the only doctor at the station so she needed to be close by, but she was also oddly comforted by the thought that Gabe would be close at hand too, especially while she familiarised herself with her strange new surroundings.

'Good decision. Staying on this floor means you'll have your own bathroom. Upstairs there are private dongas but shared facilities. You will need to keep your own bathroom clean, though. There's a roster for Saturday chores—vacuuming, cleaning common areas, shovelling snow, that sort of thing—plus everyone volunteers for a secondary position.'

'Secondary positions?'

'We all take on part-time roles in addition to normal duties. Things like librarian, firefighter, medical support team, working in the hydroponics shed or helping Dom in the kitchen. There are enough options so you should be able to choose something that interests you as long as you can do it without any extra training as we won't have time for that. But you don't need to worry about it today. I'll give you a rundown later. If you're okay, I'll leave you to get sorted. Dinner is at six and everyone will gather for a drink in the bar beforehand. Do you want me to come back for you or can you find it? It's right next to the dining hall.'

'I'll find it.'

'One last thing—it's the final bit of information for now, I promise,' he added, when Sophie suspected he'd noticed her bewildered expression. Gabe smiled at her and his dark eyes shone, and she wondered if she could think of a few questions for him, something to delay him leaving. She wasn't sure that she felt like keeping her own company but she was sure he had more important matters to attend to. 'Water is scarce over winter so we have restrictions in place.'

'Water restrictions in a place smothered in ice?' Sophie queried, thinking he had to be kidding.

'That's the problem over winter. We have plenty of ice but no water. It doesn't rain here so until the temperatures rise and the summer melt happens we have to watch our water supply. The restrictions are mainly for showers—two minutes, every second day.'

'Okay.' She hadn't been expecting that but she supposed there would be plenty more unexpected and unusual things over the next few days until she got used to her new surroundings. She closed the door behind him, letting him go. She unpacked one of her bags before deciding to explore the medical centre instead. It was her domain and she was eager to see what was in store for her.

The medical suite consisted of a consulting room, a dental and exam room, a small operating theatre, a lab, a two-bed ward, a storeroom and a bathroom. Sophie was pleasantly surprised to find the clinic so well equipped. She did a quick inventory of equipment and drugs before returning to her room. She had promised to send Luke an email to let him know she arrived safely and she figured he would have expected to hear from her by now.

She booted up her laptop and paused when the screensaver photo appeared on the display. It was a photo of Danny, taken at their wedding. The photographer had snapped it just after they'd exchanged their vows and Danny had just kissed his bride. The picture captured Danny only. He had been smiling at her, the goofy smile she had adored, and his eyes had been full of love, his dimples marking his cheeks. Sophie had loved his dimples and they had laughed about their matching genetic defects. Dimples were an inherited trait and they'd talked about passing them on to their kids. But now that wasn't to be.

She reached out and ran her fingers over the screen, tracing the angles of Danny's face, the line of his lips, the dip of his dimples. The photo stirred mixed emotions in her—love and sadness—but she couldn't bring herself to change the screensaver. She needed to see him still.

She moved her hand over the keyboard and logged onto the station's WiFi, opening up her email account before she got too maudlin. She sent Luke a quick message and promised to give more details next time when she'd had a chance to get her head around everything and had something more substantial to report or had hopefully had time to explore. It was all so different. She copied the email to the AAP division headquarters in Hobart and to her parents in Queensland to keep them in the loop. At the moment everything was very strange and new and she had no idea how to verbalise her first impressions. In a day or two things might seem less surreal.

She checked the clock and decided she had just enough time to put fresh linen on her bed and change her clothes before making her way to the bar for pre-dinner drinks. She was feeling a little homesick but knew she just needed to keep busy. She closed the laptop. She didn't need to see Danny's face right now, she needed to keep a clear head.

She eventually found her way to the bar by following the noise. It was almost full. Most of the expeditioners who hadn't left today must already be in the room. She swallowed nervously and wiped her clammy hands on her jeans. She never really liked walking into a room full of strangers.

She searched the room for a familiar face and spotted Gabe behind the bar. She headed in his direction. He saw her coming and grinned at her. Sophie returned his smile gratefully, feeling her nervousness about her new surroundings settle as she tried to fight the other butterflies that stirred in her stomach in response to Gabe's smile. She had never had such a sudden and strong reaction to any man. Danny had been familiar and comfortable. She'd

never before met a stranger who could make her go weak
at the knees with just a smile and a glance.

'What will you have?' he asked.

'What's on offer?'

'Most of the crew drink beer but most of that's brewed
here at the station over summer so it may not be to your
liking. Other than that, there's whatever we've shipped in.
There's an allowance of two drinks per day, for all sorts of
reasons, but you're welcome to one of Dr John's red wines
or one of my Tassie beers.'

'Thanks, but I think I'll stick with something soft.' She
wasn't a big drinker and while she wouldn't have minded
a glass of something to relax her she thought it was more
important to stay sober and focussed until she felt more
at ease. She was already aware that people were looking
at her with interest. She hadn't expected to be the object
of dozens of pairs of eyes all at once as she came under
the scrutiny of the entire crowd. She knew the number of
people on base shrank over winter but there were still far
more people here than she had anticipated. 'I thought most
people went home for winter?'

Gabe nodded. 'They do, but there are still thirty people
here for now. Another twelve will be heading home when
the supply ship makes its last journey before the winter
season. They've got some final packing up to do in preparation for winter and then they'll head off,' he explained.

Sophie knew the supply ship, the *Explorer Australis,*
was due to dock at Carey in six or seven weeks' time
after visiting the other two Australian Antarctic stations.
The original plan had been for Dr John to be on board, in
which case she would depart then. Until then, apparently,
she would be responsible for the thirty expeditioners who
remained on the base.

Gabe poured her a drink and then called the room to

attention. 'Everyone, I'd like you all to welcome, Sophie Thompson, our new doc.'

His introduction was followed by a chorus of 'G'day, Doc,' and Sophie suspected that from now on she was going to be known simply as 'Doc'. She didn't mind the idea—she was sure that being known as 'Doc' was preferable to being known as Danny's widow.

'You'll gradually meet everyone but for now let me introduce you to Finn,' Gabe said, as a tall, thin man approached the bar. 'Finn is our watercraft operator and along with me and Alex he's the third member of your medical support crew.'

Finn shook her hand. 'We're the important ones, Gabe, Alex and me,' he said, his greeting accompanied by a wide smile. 'We're the ones you need to know.'

He took her under his wing and proceeded to introduce her to more of the crew throughout dinner. Sophie knew it would take a few days before she would be able to put all the names and faces and their job roles together, but luckily no one seemed to expect too much of her in the way of conversation. She ate quietly, happy to watch the interaction between the expeditioners and get a feeling for the different personalities and listen to their stories. She was surprised to find that the majority of them had family at home. She hadn't realised so many would be in that situation and she wondered why they would choose to stay for months at a time if that was the case. But it seemed that many had been bitten by the Antarctic bug.

By the time dinner, a three-course affair that was apparently the norm, was finished and their dishes had been returned to the kitchen for the slushies to clean up, Sophie was exhausted. There had been a lot to absorb in the short time since she'd arrived and her eyelids were drooping as everyone made their way back to the bar. She listened to

the plans being made around her—some of the guys decided to have a jam session, others were going to watch
a movie—but Sophie just wanted to put her head down.

As soon as she thought it was polite to do so, she excused herself and went in search of her bed. Not that she
expected to sleep well but it would be wise, she thought,
to at least lie down. She hadn't had a good night's sleep
since Danny had died and she suspected that her insom-
nia would be compounded by her new surroundings and
a different bed.

Back in her donga she was glad she'd had the foresight
to make her bed. She changed into pyjamas and unpacked a
soft cashmere blanket that she had carried in her hand luggage. The blanket had once been on the bed she'd shared
with Danny and she liked to think it still smelt like him.
She knew that was fanciful thinking but it was something
that gave her some comfort. But the blanket was as much
a practical item as a comforting one. It had seemed to Sophie that she felt the cold more now that she had no one
to share her bed.

She wrapped the blanket around her shoulders and
climbed under the covers. She laid her head on her pillow
as she thought about Danny.

She knew this experience would have been right up his
alley. He had been an adrenalin junkie—not a risk-taker,
any risks he'd taken had been calculated ones—and she
knew he would have jumped at a chance to explore Antarctica. The company he and Luke had founded ran adventure tours all around Tasmania, offering everything
from white-water rafting on the Franklin River, mountain
biking down Mt Wellington, cycling the east coast, hiking on Cradle Mountain, rock-climbing and abseiling to
kayaking. His job had taken him away from home, away
from her, a lot but they had been planning on reorganis-

ing things to allow them to spend more time together as they'd hoped to start a family, but now it was just her and she had to make new plans. Solo plans. And today she had taken the first step on her new path.

'Doc?'

A voice disturbed Sophie and she rolled over, still half-asleep.

'Are you awake?'

'Hmm?'

'Doc.' The voice was a little louder this time. A little more insistent. 'You need to get up. There's been an accident.'

An accident? Danny?

Sophie's eyes flew open. There was a man standing beside her bed but he wasn't fair and clean-shaven, like Danny. He was tall and dark and bearded. He looked familiar but it still took her a moment to work out who it was.

'Gabe?'

What was he doing in her room?

There could only be one reason. She sat up.

'What is it?'

CHAPTER THREE

Date: March 8th
Temperature: -10°C
Hours of sunlight: 13.8

'WHAT'S HAPPENED?' SOPHIE asked, as she swung her legs out of bed. Gabe was standing right beside her and she tried to ignore the little frisson of excitement as she focussed on what he was saying rather than how close he stood.

'The Russians have lost a helicopter. We're sending out S&R and I need you to come with us.'

She mustn't be properly awake. It sounded as though he'd said 'Russians'.

'Russians? What Russians?'

'There's a Russian station not far from here. One of their helicopters has gone missing.'

'And you want me to go out on a search and rescue?'

He was nodding. 'Time is critical. I need you with me out in the field. We don't know what the situation is so we need to cover all contingencies—which means sending you out. I'll meet you in the medical centre. Get dressed, you'll need all your ECW gear and don't forget your goggles and gloves.'

She was wide awake now but she didn't bother asking

how you lost a helicopter. Whatever had happened couldn't be good and the only thing that mattered to her was what would be left for her to deal with. But she hadn't expected to have to deal with a crisis somewhere out on the ice, not on her first proper day on the job.

She got dressed in a hurry. The Antarctic motto of 'Hurry up and wait' didn't seem to apply to this station, she thought as she pulled on underwear, long thermals, socks, a shirt, pants and a fleece. She had her wedding ring, and Danny's, strung on a chain around her neck and she lifted the rings to her lips and kissed them, before tucking them inside her shirt.

'Wish me luck,' she whispered, as she stuffed a balaclava, goggles, sunglasses and gloves into the pocket of her fleecy jacket, before heading to the medical centre to prepare to venture into the great unknown.

Gabe, Finn and a third man were already in the clinic. She'd met the other man last night but she couldn't remember his name. So much of yesterday was a blur and she knew she would need time to get things straight in her head. Names, faces and routines would all need time to sink in but she feared she wasn't going to get that time today. Today she was going to be thrown straight in at the deep end.

Finn was standing beside a sack trolley that Sophie didn't remember having seen in the clinic before, and Gabe and the other man were gathering equipment. They weren't waiting for her. They had laid a stretcher on one of the treatment beds and had put a spinal board on top of it.

'Load anything you think you might need onto the stretcher or the trolley,' Gabe said to her as soon as she stepped into the room, 'and Liam, Finn and I will transport it for you.'

Liam, that was his name.

How did she know what to take? What would she need?

Sophie closed her eyes as she tried to focus. How did she know what she might need? How on earth was she supposed to figure that out? She'd been on the ice for less than twenty-four hours and she was terrified to think that perhaps she had taken on more than she could handle. Perhaps she wasn't ready for this.

'Are you okay?' Gabe asked.

She opened her eyes. 'Yes.' She might not think she was ready for this but she was all they had. She had to do her job. 'I admit I was hoping to start my stint down here with an easy emergency—frostbite, concussion, a broken finger, that sort of thing—but I'm okay, just trying to figure out what we'll need. You don't have any idea what we might be dealing with?'

Gabe shook his head. 'It could be anything from concussion to burns to fractures to internal injuries. Bring what you would need if you were waiting for an ambulance to bring in survivors from a train wreck. I imagine it will be similar.'

Oh, God. If she'd been waiting for multiple victims from a train wreck she would want to be in a modern emergency department with a team of nurses and surgeons on hand, a suite of theatres at her disposal, state-of-the-art X-ray facilities and a well-stocked blood bank and pharmacy. But instead she had herself. She was the doctor, the nurse, the radiologist, the anaesthetist and the pharmacist, and she was going to have to work in sub-zero temperatures bundled up like a mummy. It was a nightmare.

She knew she had a medical support team but she had no idea how well trained they were or whether or not they'd had any experience in this type of situation.

But Gabe hadn't finished. 'Best-case scenario you will

have patients to treat. Worst case—we won't find them in time.'

It wasn't just a nightmare, it was her *worst* nightmare.

But Gabe's comments jolted her back to reality. She needed to get her act together, she needed to concentrate. She couldn't afford any mistakes. Time was of the essence. They needed to get out of here. She looked around the clinic and started a mental inventory.

'How many people on board?' she asked.

'Only two.'

Good. She grabbed the emergency kit that she'd gone through yesterday and put it on Finn's trolley. It had sufficient supplies for two patients but she needed to add some more equipment. She grabbed extra blankets, an oxygen cylinder and bags of saline. She put a stethoscope around her neck and tucked it inside her thermals to keep it warm. It made a metallic chime against her wedding rings. She wrapped her fingers around the rings, squeezing them as she prayed for some luck.

What else would she need? In an ideal world she'd have some bags of blood to add to the pile but there was no blood stored. She knew that the crew would donate blood as needed but she was the only one who could take it. No one at Carey could donate blood if she wasn't there. She stood in the centre of the room while she tried to figure out what to do. She'd have to get some donors lined up for their return, just in case. She hoped someone at the station was O-negative.

'We're here to help. Tell us what you need,' Gabe said, and she knew he was trying to get her to hurry up but she was out of her depth. What she needed was reassurance.

'Have you done something like this before?' she asked.

'Not exactly,' he admitted. 'Major incidents are thankfully few and far between and we have stringent occupational health and safety policies, but we have trained for these situations and we are trained to work in these conditions.'

His confidence was reassuring. Sophie had no idea if he was as confident as he seemed but she chose to believe him. She looked up into his dark brown eyes, drawing strength from him again. She trusted him and she knew that as long as he was with her she'd feel better about the situation.

She took a deep breath. She was a doctor. She knew her trade and if she had to think on her feet she would. 'Okay, I think that's everything. We can go.' She picked up the bags of saline and the men carried everything else.

They got as far as the drying room before they had to put everything down again in order to get their final layers of clothing on. Her extreme cold-weather clothing was hanging where she'd left it yesterday.

Sophie emptied the pockets of her fleece as she'd need to wear the things she'd shoved in there. She stepped into her waterproof pants and grabbed her enormous white bunny boots. She pulled the balaclava over her head before shrugging into her red parka. She stuffed the bags of saline into her now-empty pockets, she had to be certain they didn't freeze. She could put them in the insulated emergency kit but she didn't know how it was going to be transported and she couldn't risk frozen saline. She didn't even want cold saline. She wanted it at body temperature.

She pulled her gloves on and picked up her goggles and sunglasses as Gabe picked up the emergency medical kit and opened the outer door. Flakes of snow blew into the drying room on a cold, whistling wind. Sophie pulled her balaclava over her mouth and nose and stretched her goggles over her head, before adjusting the hood of her parka. She followed Gabe outside but hesitated on the metal platform.

The world had completely disappeared. A blanket of white had been thrown over the plateau and Sophie couldn't see past the bottom of the steps. She hadn't been near a window to look outside since Gabe had woken her and she felt stunned, and a little scared, about how much had changed overnight. The wind was icy and strong— strong enough to whip the snow so that it blew past them horizontally.

As she trod carefully down the steps she could just make out the squat, red shape of a Hägglund parked beside the red shed. It was parked just a couple of metres from the base of the steps but Sophie knew she could only see it because of its colour. Visibility was almost nil but red did catch her eye. It seemed to be the colour of choice at the bottom of the world—red clothing, red buildings, red transport.

Sophie hadn't had time to think about the transportation logistics. The Hägglund sat on the snow on its caterpillar treads, looking like a mini-tank. Yesterday in the bright sunshine it had seemed exciting as it had shone brightly against the blue sky and white snow. Today in the gloomy surroundings, blanketed and buffeted by swirling snow, it seemed almost ominous.

She wondered how on earth they were going to find anything or anyone in these conditions. Some of Gabe's confidence that had rubbed off on her earlier vanished in an instant.

He turned to face her as she reached the bottom of the steps. His red jacket stood out in stark relief against the white background. Sophie looked around her, searching for landmarks, but she could see nothing other than Gabe and one Hägglund. He must have seen the look of panic on her face. 'What is it?'

'How on earth do you expect to find them in this?' she asked, waving one hand towards the snow. 'What if we get lost too?'

She thought Gabe was smiling but it was hard to tell when all she could see of his face were his dark eyes shielded by snow goggles.

'We can't get lost when we're not sure where we're going.'

'What?'

'The helicopter is lost. *We* are not. The last communication came when the chopper was about twenty kilometres west of here. We're the closest station but we don't have an exact location. We only have a last known location. Helicopters and planes can't fly in a whiteout so we have to go looking. But there's no need to panic, we have a pretty good idea of where to start.'

'And that's supposed to make me feel better?' she asked, as Gabe opened the rear door of the vehicle and indicated that she should climb on board. He put the emergency medical kit on the seat beside her and shut the door.

He climbed into the front, greeting Alex, who was in the driver's seat, before answering her question. 'We've got fifteen years of experience between us, not counting your years as a doctor. You do your job, we'll do ours. I promise I won't risk the lives of anyone on my team. That's not how this works. We've got GPS and radar tracking, we've got survival kits and all the right equipment, we have radio contact with our station and we've got the co-ordinates of the Russians' last transmission. We know where we're going and everyone back here will know where we are. We won't be lost.'

Sophie felt marginally better but her concerns about

their movements were now replaced with concern about the Russians' situation.

By Gabe's reckoning they were at least twenty kilometres away. She knew how long it had taken to cover the seventy kilometres from the airstrip to the station yesterday in clear and sunny conditions. She couldn't imagine how long it was going to take them to cover twenty kilometres, or more, in a blizzard. 'It's going to take us a while to find them, isn't it?'

Gabe nodded.

'How long have they been missing?'

'Only a little over an hour. They've missed one check-in and can't be raised on the radio.'

'And you think they might be able to survive out in these conditions for long enough for us to reach them?'

'We have to hope so. They have survival equipment on board. It all depends on what has happened—if they are injured and how badly, if the equipment has been damaged, if they can reach it and deploy it. There are a lot of variables—we have to plan for the worst and hope for the best.'

Now that she was out of the wind and snow, Sophie removed her goggles. Through the back window she could see that there was an enclosed trailer attached to the Hägglund. She could just make out the figures of Finn and Liam as they loaded her equipment into the trailer. They slammed the doors closed and disappeared. Moments later a second Hägglund, also with an attached trailer, crawled past her window on its caterpillar treads. She thought she could see Liam's profile as the tank-like vehicle moved past.

'Breakfast courtesy of Dom,' Alex said, as he passed a muffin and a travel mug of hot chocolate back to Sophie then pulled out behind the other vehicle.

'Are they coming with us?' Sophie asked, as she bit

into the muffin and inclined her head towards the other Hägglund, which was leading the way.

Gabe nodded. 'It's AAP policy that we always send out two vehicles or two boats or two helicopters. It's saved our people before but it seems that the Russians don't have the same policies. Liam is a mechanic and a firefighter and Finn is our watercraft operator, Alex is the survival expert and Finn, Alex and I are on your medical support team. We've got all bases covered. Ideally we'd send choppers out but the weather is against us on that, plus our choppers are kept at Douglas Station so even in good conditions they'd still be close to fifteen hundred kilometres from where the Russians were last heard from.'

Sophie hadn't got her head around the vastness of Antarctica. She knew the Russians had a research station about halfway between Carey and Douglas, two of the Australian stations, but if they had almost reached Carey that put them a long way from home. She wondered what had brought them so close. 'Do you know what the Russians were doing?'

'Apparently they were doing a check mission out over Bunger Hills but that would put them a long way off course if they're only twenty clicks from here. They must have had some sort of instrument failure that would put them at risk in these conditions.'

'What happens now?'

'Alex is in charge of the safety side of things. You're in charge of all things medical. We'll follow your orders but Alex has the overriding vote if he thinks there's any risk to the safety of our team. Fair enough?'

Sophie nodded. 'You said before that we plan for the worst and hope for the best. If they're dead, what do we do?'

'If we can get access we'll bring them back to the station

with us and the Russians will collect the bodies when the weather clears. The trailer attached to our Hägglund can function as an ambulance. We can transport casualties on stretchers in the back. Or fatalities in body bags if necessary.'

For someone without a medical background Gabe was very matter-of-fact but Sophie guessed that many of the seasoned expeditioners had faced all manner of testing situations that were well and truly out of the scope of normal workplace practices.

'Have you had to deal with deaths before?' she asked.

Gabe shook his head. 'Not me. But deaths aren't really the worst-case scenario. The worst case is two critically injured men out on the ice thousands of miles from a trauma centre.'

Terrific. A hundred different scenarios ran through Sophie's head. It was impossible to predict what she might need to deal with. It could be any number of things—hypothermia, fractures, spinal injuries, head or internal injuries, or a combination of all of these. And any treatment or even assessment of their potential injuries was going to be complicated by the conditions. The weather, the location and even the clothing they would be wearing would all increase the degree of difficulty.

She looked down at her own clothing. How was she going to treat them wearing these thick gloves? Could she take them off? How long would she have in these below freezing conditions before she suffered from frost-nip and then frostbite? Would there even be any point taking her gloves off to try to examine them when they would be wearing layers and layers of extreme cold-weather clothing?

Sophie had seen the immersion suits worn by anyone travelling in a helicopter that might be flying over water.

These suits were even bulkier than the cold-weather jacket and pants she wore as they had built-in flotation in case the chopper crashed into the sea. She would need to cut their suits away but that would expose them to the weather. In all her time at the other end of a phone line, advising the AMU doctors on medical matters, she hadn't had to deal with the concept of practising medicine in these extreme conditions. The job was suddenly much, much harder than she'd ever imagined.

To keep her mind focussed and her hands busy, she opened the medical kit and sorted through the contents, familiarising herself with where things were stored so she would be able to get quick access to whatever she needed. She closed her eyes and ran through the contents of the kit—bandages, syringes, drugs, suturing kits and needles—playing a version of the memory game as she tested her recall.

The visibility hadn't improved since they'd left Carey and they were making slow progress, but with her eyes closed Sophie felt the Hägglund slow even further. She opened her eyes, wondering if it was just her imagination. For a second she thought she saw a flash of red out to their right but then, just as quickly, it disappeared from view. Perhaps it was just the second vehicle. She kept her eyes on the spot, or where she thought the spot was, but she was only guessing.

A gust of wind blew the snow out of their way, clearing her sight line briefly. There it was again. Could it be the helicopter?

Before she could say anything the Hägglund ground to a halt. Through the swirling snow she could now make out the shape of the other Hägglund in front of them and she knew the glimpse of red out to the right wasn't Liam's vehicle.

'Is that the helicopter?' she asked Gabe.

'Looks like it.'

It looked nothing like it to her. It didn't resemble a helicopter at all. Was it just the weather and the poor visibility making it unrecognisable?

The snow cleared again and she could see now that it was a chopper. It was lying at an angle, slightly on its right side, like a beached whale. From this perspective it looked as though it had snapped into pieces and one rotor blade was sticking out of the snow several metres from the body of the helicopter.

She heard Gabe on the radio, advising the station that they had found the chopper. While she was listening to him she saw Liam climb out of the other vehicle. She could just make out his shape between the snow gusts. His red jacket was bright in the gaps in the snowfall and he held a long pole in his hand.

'What's Liam doing?' she asked Gabe as he ended his radio call. She wondered why they weren't moving. What were they waiting for?

'The chopper is resting on sea ice,' Gabe told her. 'We are right at the edge of the continent, where the sea ice meets the land ice. The two different bases can make the ice unstable. Where the two meet there are often cracks or fissures or crevasses. We need to check for stability so Liam is testing the snow and ice to make sure it's safe to proceed.'

Sophie was agitated. 'Can't we get out and walk?'

Gabe shook his head. 'No. It's further than it looks. Also it's minus ten degrees and blizzard conditions. What do you propose to do? Lug all your equipment with you? It will take fifteen minutes to cover that distance, without carrying any extra weight, and how will you treat him when you get there?'

'I don't know,' she said. Gabe was making sense but it was frustrating to have to sit and wait when she could see the chopper.

'If we can't drive over safely *then* we'll get out and walk,' he explained. 'But that means hauling the equipment on a sled.'

Alex opened his door and sprang out of the cab to help Liam. Icy wind blew into the vehicle, bringing with it a flurry of snow that blanketed Sophie's face. She was shocked at how frigid the air was. She'd felt quite warm in the Hägglund but she now realised it was only because she'd been sheltered from the wind.

She watched as Liam and Alex tested the ice. Liam was poking the pole into cracks in the ice while Alex appeared to be drilling into the icy crust. Liam was shorter than Alex with a more pronounced belly but both men were of similar build and it was difficult to tell them apart under the layers of clothing. From where Sophie sat Liam's moustache was the only differentiating factor, but once they were more than a few feet from the Hägglund they disappeared into the snow flurries to become only occasionally visible. She watched as one of them waved at the vehicle, motioning Gabe forward.

Gabe got on the radio again and this time spoke to Finn. 'Can we detach our trailer and put it behind yours? We'll leave our vehicle here, just in case we get into strife,' he said. He turned to Sophie. 'We'll have to swap vehicles. Rug up.'

Sophie pulled her goggles over her eyes and her hood over her head then clambered out of the Hägglund. Another blast of icy wind assaulted her and she bent almost double against the force of the gale as she made her way to the other tank-like vehicle and climbed into the back seat. Gabe placed her medical kit on the seat beside her before switching positions with Finn and taking over the driving. From the cab Sophie could see Alex attaching a cable from the Hägglund to Liam and a second one to himself.

'What are they doing?'

'Securing themselves to the Hägglund, just in case,' Gabe replied.

Sophie didn't ask any more questions. She didn't want to think about one of them falling through the ice. Liam and Alex continued to walk forward, testing the ice, with Gabe driving the vehicle and following closely behind them. They crept along slowly, inching across the ice.

Sophie opened the medical kit and selected a few essentials and stuffed them into her jacket pockets. She transferred surgical gloves, a torch and a thermometer, then checked that her stethoscope was still around her neck and that the saline bags hadn't frozen. She grabbed some IV tubing, a tourniquet and a needle, even though she had no idea how she would find a vein if she needed to run a drip—the cold weather and the layers of clothing were definitely going to make things difficult for her.

Their progress was slow and made even slower by a couple of stops to allow the men to swap places. Finn relieved Liam, who later relieved Alex, which gave them each a break and some respite from the sub-zero temperatures and strong winds.

Sophie tried to curb her impatience. The whole situation seemed quite surreal as the vehicle followed behind the men on foot and she had to remind herself that they were the experts and Gabe had promised to keep them all safe. She had to trust him and let them do their jobs. Her time was coming.

As they got nearer the chopper Sophie could see that it had broken into three pieces. The front and right-hand side was badly crumpled, the windscreen shattered but still mostly in position. The tail had broken off completely and one rotor blade had snapped off, probably on impact, and was sticking out of the snow, having been flung several metres from the helicopter.

Gabe stopped the Hägglund a few feet from the wreckage. As soon as he gave the all-clear Sophie leapt out of the cab.

'Can you bring the medical kit for me?' she asked. It was heavy and cumbersome and she knew she had the essentials she needed in her pockets. She also knew that by the time she had worked out what else she needed from the kit they would have brought it to her. She didn't need it to begin her assessment. It was more important just to get out of the vehicle.

Gabe had parked the vehicle on the right-hand side of the chopper, closest to the pilot. Sophie could see two men both still inside the chopper, their bright yellow immersion suits shining like twin beacons in the semi-darkness of the snow-covered cabin. She peered inside. The pilot was still strapped into his seat, his eyes closed. The other man's harness was undone, suggesting he must have moved at some point, but he was motionless too, eyes closed also.

Despite the damage to the helicopter, Sophie was just able to get her head and arms into the cabin and reach the pilot. He was slumped in his seat and the cabin had crushed around him. She grabbed the fingers of her thick padded gloves, ready to pull them off. She needed to feel for a pulse.

'You can't take your gloves off in this weather, Doc. Your fingers will freeze in minutes.' Gabe's voice startled her. She hadn't heard him come up behind her. The snow muffled all sound.

Sophie looked back at him. 'I can't work in these,' she said as she held her hands up. 'I have to feel for a pulse.'

'Doc, leave your gloves on.' Gabe's tone suggested that he wasn't making a request. 'You'll have to use your stethoscope.'

The pilot's immersion suit was tight around his face and neck. 'But he's got so many layers on,' she protested.

'Yuri is dead.'

Sophie's head whipped around as she looked across to the other Russian. His eyes were open now, his shallow breathing making his words faint.

'You speak English?'

'Da.'

'Have you checked him?' Sophie could see no evidence that the pilot had been checked or that the passenger had moved. He didn't appear to have tried to reach any of the survival gear and Sophie wondered if he'd tried to help the pilot—Yuri. What had happened?

'Nyet. I cannot move. My foot, it is stuck. But Yuri has not moved either.'

Sophie realised it didn't matter to her what had happened, what had gone on before they'd reached the scene. What mattered now was sorting out the casualties. She needed to prioritise but triage was a problem. She was used to casualties being brought in by ambulance. Usually the paramedics would give some indication of a patient's condition, which would make triage much easier. But out here there was no one who could tell her what the state of play was. It was up to her.

The passenger was conscious and coherent. The pilot was unresponsive. According to the passenger, the pilot was dead but Sophie wasn't prepared to accept his diagnosis. She needed to confirm that for herself. She knew he could be dead but he could also be hypothermic and, therefore, potentially in more need of help.

'Are you hurt?' she asked, directing her question to the passenger.

'My foot and my back.'

'Can you see if you can free his foot?' Sophie asked Gabe. It would buy her a few minutes with the pilot if Gabe could check out the passenger. He nodded and made his way around the front of the helicopter.

Sophie felt in her pocket for her torch while she spoke to Yuri. She wanted him to know what was going on just in case he could hear her. 'Yuri, I'm a doctor. I'm just going to open your eyes.'

Sophie tried to gently push up one of his eyelids, only to find it didn't move. It was frozen shut.

She checked the time. It was a little over two hours since the helicopter had been reported missing. In these sub-zero temperatures rigor mortis could have already started to set in and the muscles of the eyelids were one of the first to show the signs. But, then again, it could just be that Yuri's eyelids had frozen shut.

She'd heard about this happening but had never experienced it.

She opened the medical chest that Gabe had left at her side, pleased that whoever had designed it had had the foresight to make sure it could be easily opened while wearing gloves, and found the eye solution. 'Yuri, I'm going to wipe your eyes to get them open.' She poured some saline onto a gauze dressing and wiped the cloth across Yuri's eyelids. She didn't want to leave any moisture on his skin, knowing it would freeze solid again, but she needed to melt the ice that had frozen on his lids.

She flicked on the torch before lifting Yuri's eyelids, relieved to find that this time she was able to prise them open, and shone the torch briefly into first one eye and then the other. His pupils didn't react. They were fixed and dilated. It didn't help her with a diagnosis, all it told her was that his condition wasn't good.

Yuri could have a head injury but severe hypothermia could have the same affect.

Or he could be dead.

She untucked the stethoscope from her jacket and popped it in her ears. Because Yuri was slumped in his seat, she couldn't unzip his immersion suit to reach his chest. She held the stethoscope against his carotid artery listening in vain for a heart beat.

Nothing.

She took the stethoscope and held the round, silver disc under Yuri's nose, searching for condensation, looking for a sign that he was breathing.

Still nothing. But she still refused to believe it was all over for Yuri. Maybe he was just cold. She knew that in severe cases of hypothermia a person's heartbeat and respiration dropped and could be as slow as one to two per minute.

From across the cabin of the chopper she could see Gabe watching her, a question in his brown eyes.

'He could be hypothermic,' she said, refusing to give up until she'd checked Yuri more thoroughly. 'I need to get them both out.'

'We'll have to cut them out,' Gabe told her. 'Who do you want to move first?'

Sophie was nervous. She knew it was her call but the decision wasn't an easy one. Yuri's condition was potentially more critical—if he was still alive. But even if he was alive she knew that her treatment options for him were limited out here on the ice. They couldn't afford to spend precious time extricating Yuri in case the passenger's condition deteriorated. Time was valuable. She needed to get them somewhere warm. And that presented another problem.

Where could she treat them?

'Where will we put them?' she asked.

'The trailer that we brought is set up like an ambulance but you won't have much room to manoeuvre in there with two patients. The other trailer is full of safety gear,' Gabe said. 'We can set up a bivvy—a bivouac tent,' he clarified for her benefit, 'and put them in there. Who do you want moved first?' he repeated.

'Your guy.'

It was her job to save lives. There were two patients who needed her but she knew for certain that one was still alive. She couldn't afford to risk his life by making the wrong choice. She'd made her decision but still found herself looking to Gabe for confirmation. She needed his reassurance.

Gabe's brown eyes anchored her, once again settling her nerves, and she decided she preferred goggles to sunglasses. The goggles didn't hide his eyes and his eyes gave her the strength she needed. He nodded his head slightly, giving her the reassurance she sought, and she could see why he held the position of Station Leader. His quiet, calm manner would get the best out of his people.

Alex, Finn and Liam sprang into action. They had assembled a pile of gear in the snow beside the chopper. Sophie recognised metal cutters, stretchers and tarpaulins amongst the other paraphernalia.

She moved around to the other side of the chopper while the men got things organised. She let them do their jobs. There was nothing more she could do with Yuri until he was freed.

'I'm the doctor,' she said to the other man. She didn't bother to give her name. The new nickname was giving her the chance to escape the past. A chance to be someone other than Sophie, Danny's widow. 'What is your name?'

'Nikolai.'

She desperately wanted to check Nikolai's vital signs. She wanted to take his blood pressure and check his heart rate and oxygen sats, but in order to do that she needed access to his arm, wrist and fingers, and she couldn't risk exposing him to the hostile elements. She had to be content with the fact that he was alert and responsive and assume that any injuries he'd sustained weren't life-threatening. She'd need to be patient and wait until the guys had freed him from the wreckage so she resigned herself to keeping conversation going instead, making sure she kept Nikolai focussed and awake. 'Do you remember what happened?'

'Nyet.'

'Did you hit your head? Lose consciousness at all?' He looked at her blankly until she added, 'Did you black out?'

'Maybe,' he replied, and Sophie gave up her questioning. Between his possible memory loss and their language incompatibility she figured she wasn't going to get anywhere.

She stepped aside as Alex cut part of the chopper away to free Nikolai's foot. Finn was spreading a tarp on the ground as Liam and Alex pulled at the metal, twisting it out of the way and opening up some space around Nikolai's legs.

'We're clear,' Alex said.

'Ready to lift?' Gabe asked.

Sophie looked around. 'Wait! Where are you going to put him? The tent isn't up.'

'Don't worry, Doc, the bivvy will go up around you,' Gabe told her, then turned back to Alex. 'On three.'

'It's going to hurt,' Sophie told Nikolai as Gabe counted them down to the lift.

'Is okay,' the Russian replied.

'One, two, three.'

Gabe and Alex lifted Nikolai out of the chopper and Sophie saw what little colour he'd had drain from his face. Finn had placed a space blanket and the medical chest on the tarpaulin and Gabe and Alex laid Nikolai down then immediately returned to the chopper to finish cutting Yuri out.

Sophie knelt beside Nikolai and before she could ask any more questions or wonder about the wisdom of moving her patient before the tent was erected Finn had pulled a tent over the top of them all. Within seconds he had cocooned them from the wind and snow, sheltering them from the elements.

Sophie was amazed. There wasn't room to stand in the tent but it served as a perfectly adequate shelter. In order to keep its shape it needed someone to lean against the sides but Finn was able to do that while she turned her attention to Nikolai.

She barely had time to open the medical chest and begin to assess Nikolai when Gabe crawled into the tent through the small door. Sophie was immediately aware of his presence and it wasn't just because of the way he filled the space inside the tent. There was enough room in there for half a dozen bodies but his presence seemed to charge the air around her. She could feel the air shift and stir as Gabe moved, almost as though it breathed with him. It made no sense to be so aware of him, she knew nothing about him, he was just a man, yet she was far more aware of him than she was of anyone else out there today.

'Yuri is almost out,' he told her. 'We'll put him in the Hägglund when he's freed.'

'Shouldn't I check him in here?' she asked, but Gabe's expression told her he thought she was wasting her time and for a moment she figured he probably knew more about Yuri's chances than she did. She'd only ever dealt with mild cases of hypothermia before but she still wasn't prepared to write him off just yet. 'Just in case? There's more space.'

Gabe shook his head. 'There was no chance of saving him, he was dead before we got here.'

Sophie knew Gabe was trying to make her feel better about the choices she'd made but she still felt her chest contract with guilt. A man was dead.

But she couldn't afford to dwell on Yuri now. She'd deal with that later. Right now she needed to concentrate on Nikolai.

Gabe was squatting beside her and his proximity was distracting her. She tried to block out her awareness of him, she needed to focus, but she didn't want to ignore him completely. Having him nearby made her feel positive. His presence gave her confidence and let her think that maybe things would be okay.

Now that she was shielded from the worst of the weather she could feel her body temperature begin to rise and she was willing to risk removing her gloves. She tucked them into her pocket and swapped them for a pair of surgical gloves. She opened the medical chest and rummaged for a pair of scissors, placing them on the top of the chest.

She turned to Gabe. 'Have we got spare clothes?' she asked.

He nodded. 'There'll be a survival kit in the helicopter if I can get to it.'

'And if you can't?'

'We have sleeping bags. They are just as effective at maintaining heat and easier to use. I'll bring you whatever I can find,' he said, starting to crawl back out of the tent.

'Can you bring the oxygen cylinder too?' she called after him.

Sophie didn't want to undress Nikolai too much until

Gabe had brought things to keep him warm, but she needed to start with the basics. She took one of his gloves off and popped an oximeter on his finger and took his temperature using a tympanic thermometer. She spoke to him quietly, explaining what she was doing. He didn't say much and she had no idea whether he understood anything she told him or if he was in shock and unable to comprehend what was going on.

His oxygen sats were low and so was his core temperature. She picked up the scissors and slit his immersion suit from his wrist to his elbow and wrapped a blood-pressure cuff around his arm. His pulse rate was fast and his blood pressure was low. Sophie opened the top of his suit and lifted his shirt to expose his chest. She put her stethoscope on his skin and listened for equal air entry, relieved to find his chest sounds were normal.

If asked for a diagnosis she knew he had sustained orthopaedic injuries and she suspected he had internal injuries as well, coupled with hypothermia, but she couldn't assess much more without better access. She took comfort from the fact that his vital signs, while not great, weren't critical yet, and unless he did have severe internal injuries her gut feeling was that he would probably pull through.

She palpated his abdomen while she waited for Gabe. Nikolai didn't report any tenderness with that but he did complain of back pain. She couldn't examine his back without moving him and she was reluctant to do that until she'd assessed his leg. It was a bit of a Catch-22 situation but, knowing that hypothermic patients should be kept as still as possible, she erred on the side of caution and pulled his shirt down again, trying to keep him warm.

She heard rustling as someone crawled back in through the opening of the tent. She felt the air stir and knew it was Gabe. Now she could check Nikolai's leg. Using the scissors, she slit the rubber immersion suit from his ankle to his groin.

'Doc!'

Sophie glanced across at Gabe. 'What?' she asked, as she peeled open the leg of Nikolai's suit.

Gabe gestured at Nikolai's now destroyed suit. 'Those suits cost thousands of dollars.'

Sophie shrugged. It was too late to worry about that. Even if she'd known their value she wouldn't have cared— her patient came first. 'There's more to worry about than the price of a suit,' she said, as she looked at Nikolai's leg. He'd fractured his tibia just above the ankle, his calf was swollen and bruised and she could see the bulge where the bone had snapped but hadn't broken through the skin. She ran her fingers gently over his leg and saw him grimace with pain at her touch. She could hear crepitus as the bone ends rubbed together, confirming her initial diagnosis. She pressed her fingers behind his ankle and was relieved to feel a pulse.

Now that Gabe was back with the sleeping bags she could risk uncovering Nikolai's chest and upper limbs to begin treating his hypothermia and finish her examination. She was just beginning to think she could work with Gabe without losing her focus when he passed her a sleeping bag and their fingers touched. He had removed his gloves and through the thin rubber of her surgical gloves Sophie could feel the heat of his hands. The warmth took her by surprise and she paused as the heat flooded through her. It was odd how she could feel it flow through her body until it pooled in her belly. She felt as though she was being wrapped in a warm hug and the sensation made her catch her breath.

But she was being ridiculous. A reaction like hers was totally out of proportion to a simple touch of a hand. She blamed the adrenalin that she knew would be coursing through her system. It was ridiculous to think what she was feeling had anything to do with Gabe. Her blood would be full of adrenalin. The whole situation was unusual and highly stressful—it was no wonder her senses and reactions were heightened.

She refocussed, concentrating hard to remember what she was about to do as she opened the sleeping bag out and laid it over Nikolai's legs. She'd come back to that fracture later. She'd need to X-ray it and set it but splinting would be the best she could do for now. Anything further would have to wait until they were back at the station. But before she attempted to splint his leg she wanted to administer some pain relief and begin trying to combat his hypothermia.

She connected tubing and an oxygen mask to the cylinder that Gabe placed beside her and slipped the mask over Nikolai's nose and mouth. She needed to get access to a vein in order to start an infusion of warm saline solution to increase his body temperature. She hoped she'd managed to keep the saline solution warm enough with her own body heat. She prepared the bag and the tubing, checking for air bubbles, before handing the bag to Gabe.

'Can you tuck this inside your suit to keep it warm and kneel up as high as you can to keep it elevated?' she asked him. They were restricted by the close confines of the tent but she needed the bag to be elevated and the saline to stay as warm as possible.

Gabe took the bag and Sophie returned her attention to the task at hand, managing to get vein access relatively easily considering the temperature. She made sure the saline was flowing before drawing up some pain relief. He would need it before they moved him.

'Are you allergic to anything?' she asked, hoping his English was good enough to understand her question.

'Anyone with allergies has to wear a MedicAlert bracelet while they're on the ice,' Gabe told her. She'd forgotten that and she hadn't noticed a bracelet when she'd cut Nikolai's suit but she double-checked to make sure as Nikolai shook his head. Satisfied, she drew up the pain relief and injected it into the IV line.

She opened a second sleeping bag and covered Nikolai's torso, making sure to cover his head as well before turning her attention to his leg. She splinted it as quickly and as best she could and had just finished when Alex stuck his head into the tent.

'Yuri is in the Hägglund. Let us know when you're ready to move Nikolai.'

There was so much going on and Sophie could only hope she was on top of it all. Thankfully the others all seemed to be taking things in their stride and doing what needed to be done. Liam, Gabe and Alex were taking care of the logistics and the evacuation and leaving her to worry about the medical aspects of the exercise. They seemed to be working smoothly with no outward sign that things were out of control and she had to trust that they knew what they were doing.

She nodded and turned to Gabe. 'Do you think you can get Nikolai onto a stretcher? I need to check Yuri, I have to confirm his condition.' She waited for a nod from him before she crawled out of the tent. She shoved her hands into her pockets to keep them warm as she left Alex to help Gabe as she made her way to the Hägglund. At some point the vehicle had been moved and was now only a few steps from the bivouac tent, but just those few steps were enough for her to feel the cold bite of the weather.

She climbed into the vehicle and knelt beside the bench seat where Alex and Liam had put Yuri. She was no longer able to open his eyes so she opened the front of his immersion suit instead. But it didn't take her long to come to the same decision as the others.

Yuri's skin was icy to touch, his core temperature was twenty-eight degrees Celsius and his limbs were stiff. Sophie knew her findings still didn't rule out severe hypothermia—unconsciousness would occur at about thirty degrees and his limb stiffness could be rigor mortis or it could just be the cold—but even she had to admit his condition didn't look promising. She found nothing to suggest that he might be able to be revived. It was too cold and it had been too long. She listened to his chest for a couple of minutes, hoping for any sound, a heartbeat, a breath, but it was in vain. There was nothing.

She hadn't wanted to believe that he was dead but she had to admit defeat.

Her first full day on the ice and she already had a death. She knew it wasn't her fault but that didn't stop the guilt.

She sat back on her heels. Lost. Beaten. Defeated.

She looked at Yuri's face as he lay unmoving before her and for a brief moment all she could see was Danny. All she could remember was the moment when she'd had to formally identify his body.

Physically Yuri didn't resemble Danny at all. Yuri was darker and older, with lined and weathered skin. Danny had still been a boy by comparison, and in Sophie's mind Danny would always be young, but he and Yuri had something in common now. They were both dead.

Deep down she knew she'd had no chance of saving either of them but that didn't stop the memories from flooding back. What if she hadn't taken the extra shift that day? What if she and Danny had gone out for breakfast as they'd planned? They'd been talking about spending more time together—why hadn't she said no to work? Why hadn't Danny been more important?

She knew why. They'd thought they would have a life-time together. What did one day matter when you had the rest of your lives?

She wouldn't make that mistake twice.

CHAPTER FOUR

'DOC? ARE YOU OKAY?' Gabe's voice interrupted her guilty reminiscing.

She could see the worry in his eyes but she couldn't answer him. Not yet. Not until she got the image of Danny out of her head. She nodded.

'Are you sure?' he added.

Was he worried about her or concerned that she couldn't do her job? Did he think she was falling apart? Was he worried about her state of mind?

She had to reassure him. She knew she needed to push on. She couldn't sit here wallowing in the past. There were still people relying on her. Nikolai for starters.

'Yes.' She reached up and took the saline bag from Gabe and hung it on a hook that was sticking out of the Hägglund's roof as Gabe and Alex slid Nikolai's stretcher into the trailer. She needed to keep moving. She needed to keep busy. She knew from experience that if her mind was busy she didn't have time to dwell on Danny.

With an elaborate rope and pulley system, Gabe and Alex stabilised Nikolai's stretcher in the makeshift ambulance as Sophie secured the oxygen cylinder. Once they were finished there was just enough room for her to squeeze in too.

'What happens now?' she asked.

'We'll head back to Carey and when the weather clears the Russians will come to collect them. You'll be responsible for Nikolai until then. Are you going to be all right in here for the trip back?'

'Yes.' She didn't have any option. There was no room for anyone else once the medical chest and other equipment had been stowed in the trailer with her. Finn handed her a couple of energy bars and a bottle of water and Gabe showed her how to use the intercom to communicate with the front cab if she needed to, but other than one stop to let Finn and Liam out to collect the other Hägglund the return trip went without incident.

By the time they reached Carey Sophie was exhausted and she wondered if this was going to be permanent state for her while she was on the ice but, then again, her first proper day on the job had been beyond stressful. It had required massive levels of concentration and she'd had no respite. Being the sole doctor for hundreds of miles was no picnic.

There were plenty of willing hands to help unload the Hägglunds when they returned to the station but it was her Russian patients that Sophie was concerned with. Nikolai was her first priority and he was transferred immediately from the vehicle to the medical centre but she was unsure what the procedure was for the pilot.

'What happens to Yuri?' she asked Gabe. 'Do we have a morgue?' She couldn't remember seeing a morgue, there certainly wasn't one attached to the medical centre, which would have been the obvious place, but she knew she'd only seen a fraction of the red shed and who knew what was housed in some of the other station buildings.

'Not as such,' Gabe replied. 'We'll have to freeze him in a body bag and wait for the Russians to collect him.'

That sounded a bit archaic but she supposed it was the way things were done and she wasn't about to argue. She couldn't pretend to be up to speed with all the procedural ins and outs and she had other priorities. 'No post-mortem?' she queried.

Gabe shook his head. 'I'm the coroner for our station but you pronounced Yuri dead at the scene, which is out of my jurisdiction so the Russians will take care of that.'

Sophie was relieved. She didn't think her skills extended to conducting an autopsy. All she could do for Yuri now was to prepare his body. It wasn't an urgent task but she wanted to do that before he was zipped into a body bag and taken away.

'Can Yuri be brought to the medical centre too?' she asked, 'I'd like to clean him before we freeze him.'

'Sure, Doc. I'll send Alex and Finn to help you if you think that's enough hands. I need to put in a call to update the Russians on the situation.'

Sophie nodded. Nikolai was waiting for her. Yuri too. She needed to get moving.

X-rays of Nikolai's leg confirmed a slightly displaced simple tibial fracture. Sophie sedated him before realigning it and Finn had helped her to put a cast on it. Sophie wasn't too concerned about the fracture; of more concern was the blood that appeared in his urine. On examination she suspected bruised kidneys, and when Alex told her that Nikolai's seat in the chopper had snapped at the base that confirmed her diagnosis and she felt marginally happier with his condition.

Alex, Finn and Sophie worked tirelessly to get Nikolai sorted and when they eventually had him stable, fed and resting in one of the two beds in the small ward room Sophie turned her attention to Yuri. She undressed and bathed him, examining his body for signs of injury. But apart from some bruising on his chest and abdomen there were no other visible signs and she suspected he must have died from internal injuries. But it wasn't her role to determine the cause of the death or to investigate the accident. Her job was difficult enough and she had no desire to complicate it further.

When she had finished tending to Yuri Alex and Finn zipped him into a body bag and took him out of the clinic. She didn't ask where they would take him, she didn't think she needed to know, and there was enough going on in her head already.

Finding herself alone for the first time that day, she was tempted to sit down but thought she might never get up again. She could feel fatigue starting to take hold. Her legs were wobbly and her head was light. She needed to eat something but she didn't want to leave Nikolai. To distract herself and her stomach, she checked his obs and tidied the clinic. If she kept busy she wouldn't be able to fall asleep. She was putting the last few items away in a cupboard when the clinic door opened and Gabe appeared.

'How's it going?' he asked, as she straightened up and shut the cupboard door.

Her energy level lifted. Maybe it was just having some company again, someone to talk to, but she seemed to have an immediate reaction to Gabe that she didn't notice with any of the others. His energy seemed to flow to her and she felt as though it could sustain her. 'Okay,' she replied. 'I'm under control, I think. Have you spoken to the Russians?'

'I have,' he said, as he perched on the edge of her desk. 'They will come to fetch Yuri's body and Nikolai when the weather clears, if you give Nikolai the okay to travel. Their doctor has asked for an update on his condition so I told them you'd call when you can.'

'I'll talk to him now.' She may as well get it done now.

She suspected the Russian doctor would be keen to hear from her—she knew she would be sitting by the phone if the situation were reversed. She crossed to her desk, only realising as she reached for the phone that Gabe was practically sitting on it. He didn't move.

He took up a lot of room. The room was small to begin with and Gabe seemed to fill most of the available space. She could feel her stomach fluttering as she reached for the phone. Goose-bumps covered her skin, making the hairs on her arms stand up.

Gabe finally stood up as he gave Sophie the number. He waited while she'd made the call but at least he didn't remain sitting on her desk. He moved just far enough away to enable her to concentrate but she was still aware of his whereabouts as he wandered through the clinic and into the ward room. Her eyes followed his movements and even as she spoke to the Russian doctor she kept Gabe in the corner of her vision. Through the open door she saw him stop at Nikolai's bedside before he returned to the clinic room.

'Do you want to go and grab some dinner and a shower?' he asked, as she hung up the phone.

She managed a smile. 'I thought we were only allowed to shower every second day? I don't think I qualify for one yet.'

'Oh, I think you've earned it, and as the station leader I can grant favours.'

'Really?'

'Of course. There have to be some perks to the job or no one would take it on.' Gabe smiled at her, his teeth a startling white in the dark shadow of his beard, and Sophie's body sprang to attention. She'd thought he exuded a sense of calm confidence but when he smiled at her she felt anything but calm. Her heart raced in her chest, her palms sweated and her breathing was shallow. She was in equal parts nervous, excited and self-conscious. It was purely a physical reaction but thankfully Gabe didn't seem to notice her discomfort. He continued, 'I'm sure you could do with a break.'

As tempting as it was, Sophie was reluctant to go. 'It does sound good but I don't really want to leave Nikolai.' She didn't want to leave Nikolai or Gabe.

'I'll stay with him. I can call you over the intercom system if I need you. You'll only be a few steps away.'

Sophie was still finding her feet on her first proper day. She'd hate to abdicate responsibility and have something go wrong. 'Thanks for the offer but I think I'll stay here and I might put that favour in the bank for when I could really use one.'

'I'll bring dinner to you, then. What about Nikolai? Can he eat?'

Sophie glanced at the sleeping form of the Russian. He was sedated and seemed to be sleeping peacefully. 'He's had some soup,' she said. 'It's probably better to leave him sleeping.'

Gabe returned within minutes, carrying a tray of food, which he put onto her desk.

'It smells fantastic.' She was starving. She'd had nothing but a couple of energy bars since her take-away breakfast and now that she could smell dinner she could no longer distract her stomach or her brain from the idea of eating.

'Pumpkin soup and mushroom risotto,' Gabe said, as he removed the cloches covering the dishes with a flourish.

Sophie could see two servings of soup and risotto on the tray. Was he planning on eating with her?

Her earlier nervousness returned. The butterflies in her stomach had been getting a lot of exercise since she'd arrived in Antarctica. She'd expected some nerves with regard to her surroundings and the work, but her reaction to Gabe was unexpected and she wasn't sure what to do about it. And she definitely wasn't sure if spending time alone with him was a good idea. He flustered her. Actually, that wasn't quite true—her reaction to him flustered her.

She decided not to jump to conclusions. Perhaps he wasn't staying. Perhaps he had work to do. Perhaps he was going to deliver her meal and then take his to his own office. She lifted two bowls for herself off the tray and sat at her desk. Gabe grabbed a second chair, pulled it over to the desk and sat down too. It looked like he was planning on eating with her.

'You don't need to stay. Why don't you eat in the dining room with everyone else?'

'Because I thought that after the day we've had you might like some company. Was I wrong? Would you rather be alone?'

'No, not at all.' She didn't want him to go and although his presence unsettled her she preferred the idea of his company over being alone. She'd had enough of being alone.

'All right, then.' He picked up a linen napkin and shook it open before placing it gently across her lap. Sophie froze as his hand brushed her thigh. Even through the thin fabric of her scrubs she could feel his body heat and the sensation tied her tongue in knots as she struggled to make conversation. But her brain seemed to have shut down for the day, which wasn't surprising given the day she'd had, but it did leave her feeling at a distinct disadvantage.

His presence put knots in more places than just her tongue. Her stomach was doing so many somersaults she wasn't sure if she was going to be able to eat, despite the fact that she was starving. She didn't know what to think about Gabe yet or about the reaction he provoked in her. She didn't want to be so aware of him. She wanted to be neutral. She wanted to be Switzerland. She didn't want to find him attractive but that was exactly what was happening. She didn't know what it was yet—his strength? His eyes? His solidness? He seemed dependable and he gave her confidence in this unfamiliar environment. But it was more than confidence. Having him nearby heightened her senses and she realised then what it was.

He made her feel alive.

He passed her some cutlery and her fingers brushed against his as she took the silverware from his hand, sending another burst of energy through her, and this time she couldn't pass it off as adrenalin or fatigue.

It was attraction.

It was absurd. She'd known him for barely twenty-four hours, yet she couldn't deny what she was feeling. Her hands were shaking, her stomach was tied up in knots and her pulse was racing. Gabe stirred her senses.

She couldn't deny it but she could try to ignore it.

It was way too soon to find another man attractive. Even though it was obvious she wasn't getting a say in the matter—her body was making its own decisions. It wasn't her fault but it was still trouble.

She snatched her hand back and unwrapped her cutlery, breaking eye contact, and spooned up some soup as she willed her hands to quit shaking. She wasn't even sure if she could eat. It was hard to swallow when it felt like all the air was being squeezed from her lungs.

But Gabe seemed unfazed. 'You coped really well today,' he said as he stirred his soup.

'I'm not sure that Yuri would agree.' Sophie hadn't had a chance to process how she felt about Yuri's demise. She knew she couldn't have changed the outcome but that didn't seem to stop the guilt.

'Please, don't blame yourself for that. We were too

late. There was nothing you could have done. You have to agree.'

'Maybe. But that doesn't change the fact that someone died today.'

'Agreed. But it wasn't of our doing. You should focus on the things that went right. Nikolai is going to be okay, thanks to you. Today was a challenge but I thought you were remarkable.'

His comment brought a smile to her lips. How was it that he knew exactly the right thing to say?

She wanted to challenge herself and today had certainly been a challenge, both mentally and physically. She'd been worried at times about being out of her depth, and to know that Gabe thought she'd handled the situation well was reassuring. She hadn't thought she was one who looked for approval but Gabe's compliment helped to assuage her guilt.

'Although I don't imagine that's how you pictured your first day would go?' he added.

She shook her head. 'No. Please, tell me that today was out of the ordinary.' Being challenged like this on occasions was fine, but she didn't think she wanted to have days like this constantly.

'Definitely extraordinary. I've never had a day like it in the three years I've been here.'

'You all seemed to cope with it better than me.'

Gabe shrugged. 'We've had plenty of training and we're used to these conditions. Everything was new for you. I had hoped to organise some field training for you before you had to experience a real emergency but obviously that went out the window. But I promise we'll do it as soon as we get a decent day.'

'Barring any other emergencies.'

'Yes.' He smiled at her and his chocolate-brown eyes

shone and it felt like the temperature in the room rose another couple of degrees.

Sophie finished her soup and pushed it to one side, ready to make a start on the risotto. 'You've been here for three years? This is a long-term proposition for you?'

'Not three years continuously but this is my third stint and it's getting close to a total of three years. There's a saying on the ice that goes something like this. The first time you come to Antarctica is for the adventure, the second time is for the money and the third time is because you can't work anywhere else.'

'And is that right?'

'Pretty much. Although I don't know about the money part. I spent many years working on mine sites and the money is better there. And you get more time off. But I've chosen to come back here when I could easily have gone back on the mines, so I guess I must like it.'

'What do you like about it?'

'It's the last frontier. It's a beautiful place but it can be hostile. It will test your wits and your endurance but I like the challenge. Working on the mines was interesting but after a while it became mundane. Being here is definitely not about the money. It's been a huge adventure and I'm afraid it's rather addictive.'

'You don't mind being here for months at a time?'

'Not at all.'

'Do you miss your family?'

'I don't have any.'

'No one?' Everyone had someone, didn't they? But Gabe was shaking his head.

'That's another reason why this suits me. These guys are like family to me. There are a few of us who have done several stints together and you become pretty close.'

Sophie wondered how close he was with other members

of the crew. He had a lone-wolf aura about him, seeming to stand apart, but she wondered if that was something she projected onto him. Maybe it was more of an alpha-wolf thing, not a lone wolf. She'd seen how the others responded to him—the S&R team and the general crew last night when Gabe had been behind the bar—there was respect and a bond so perhaps alpha wolf was a better description. Even she was falling under his spell.

'What did you do on the mines?'

'I was a chef.'

'Really?'

'I was called a cook but I trained as a chef.'

'How long did you work there for?'

'Eight years with a year off in the middle when I went to work on a cattle station and I came here when I was twenty-eight.'

'To work as a chef?'

'No. I wanted a change and the Antarctic programme appealed to me but there wasn't a chef's position at the time so I worked as a storeman first.'

'And now you're the station leader.' Sophie suspected a lot of drive and determination lay behind his calm exterior.

'Yep.'

'How do you go from being a chef in the mines to a station leader in Antarctica? They seem like polar opposites—' Sophie broke off when Gabe raised one eyebrow and she realised what she'd said. 'Pardon the pun.'

He grinned at her and the force of his smile distracted her from thoughts of her accidental pun.

'There's a lot of downtime with mining rosters. Most mines run a two-week-on, two-week-off roster. The guys with families spend their weeks off at home, doing family things. I spent my time off studying and getting as many qualifications and certificates as I could.'

'What did you need?'

'For the storeman's job not much—a driver's licence, first aid and CPR qualifications—but my additional licences helped me get the station leader role. The AAP was more interested in people management skills and on paper I was probably overqualified for the job. I ran the kitchen at the last mine site, which was a big operation, but all the extra things might have made the difference between me and the next candidate.'

'What sort of extra things?'"

'My OH&S experience, forklift and truck licences, boat licence, and now I'm the policeman, coroner and station counsellor as well.'

'Are you a type-A personality or just a regular over-achiever?'

Gabe laughed and his deep, rich voice vibrated through her. 'I'm a late bloomer. It took me a while to work out what I wanted to do with my life. How about you? Did you always want to become a doctor?'

'Pretty much,' she said, as she swallowed the last mouthful of her risotto. It was creamy and full of flavour. 'That was delicious.'

'Dom's a genius in the kitchen. Good food is such a morale booster, especially over winter.'

'I didn't really expect to have fresh vegetables in my meal.'

'The mushrooms are grown in our hydroponics shed.'

'Do you grow all your vegetables here?'

'No. We couldn't keep up with the demand when the station is at capacity over the summer months but that's okay because fruit and veg can be flown in then. But we can grow enough to supply the smaller winter crew and the shed is a popular option on the volunteer roster for the winter expeditioners—it's warm and has constant light, which is a nice contrast to the winter conditions on the ice,' he said, as he picked up their plates. 'Shall I bring back some dessert or do you want to take a break and head to the mess room?'

'No, if it's okay I'll stay here, I need to take Nikolai's obs.'

Sophie pushed her chair back and went into the ward room. She could feel her eyelids drooping as she checked Nikolai and recorded her readings. The warmth of the room and the fullness of her belly was a soporific combination and the other hospital bed was beckoning. Surely it wouldn't hurt to put her head on the pillow for a couple of minutes while she waited for dessert? She stretched out on top of the sheets and closed her eyes. She just needed a few quiet moments to make sense of the day.

Alex had offered to take dessert to Sophie but Gabe had insisted that he didn't mind. Despite the mountain of paperwork that faced him after the day's events, he had no desire to sit at his desk. Sophie was like a breath of fresh air to the station. To him. And it had been a long time since he'd felt an attraction to someone. He knew it was dangerous but he was drawn to her and his desk and the pile of paperwork couldn't compete with his desire to spend a little more time in her company. He knew he wasn't thinking with his head, he knew he was headed for trouble, but he couldn't resist.

He pushed open the clinic room door, only to discover Sophie fast asleep on the spare bed in the two-bed ward. She was lying on top of the sheets and he could only assume she hadn't intended to doze off, but he wasn't surprised. Today would have been stressful for her, it was no wonder she was exhausted. But she'd coped really well with the drama. He had known she'd been nervous—that was completely reasonable—but she'd held it together. He knew from her file that she had emergency-room experience but no field experience. She hadn't been a medic in the defence force, like many other polar medicine doctors, including Dr John, had been.

He watched her as she slept. She was wearing a set of navy blue surgical scrubs that made her skin look pale and perfect and she had striped thermal socks on her feet. On one of her cheeks there was still a light dusting of powder that he suspected had come from the surgical gloves. He'd wanted to reach out and brush it off while they ate dinner but had decided against it. It was endearing to him that she hadn't noticed it and he knew that by wiping it away he was just looking for an excuse to touch her and that would have seemed far too familiar.

She had pulled her dark hair into a ponytail but some wisps had escaped from the elastic and curled around her face. He searched for signs of her dimples but they'd disappeared while she slept. She looked peaceful but, in his opinion, still too thin.

The station was heated to twenty degrees Celsius year round, a comfortable temperature usually, but he wasn't sure how warm the scrubs were and he suspected that with no meat on her bones she would feel the cold. He wondered if he should wake her and send her to bed but realised she would probably want to stay in the clinic to keep an eye on Nikolai. He grabbed a blanket instead and draped it over her, hoping she would be okay. He was reluctant to leave her but he knew it would seem odd if he stayed. There was no reason for him to keep watch over her but he felt an unusual sense of guardianship. She seemed vulnerable and delicate, although he knew she wasn't. He'd seen her strength today so it was obviously just a sense he got while she was sleeping.

She was an odd mixture of fragility and strength. Her fragility brought out his protective instincts, even though she wasn't his to protect, and she was unlikely to ever be, but he couldn't deny that he'd felt a spark of attraction today. No surprise really. She was an attractive woman, but the spark had been more than simple curiosity.

Maybe it had just been the circumstances. Maybe the drama today had served to bond them. Perhaps that connection he believed he'd felt hadn't been chemistry. Perhaps it was nothing more than a shared experience. But it didn't feel like nothing and he couldn't ignore it completely, no matter how hard he told himself to.

He needed to walk away.

Perhaps he could pretend the attraction didn't exist. Perhaps if he could ignore it, it would go away. He wasn't one to play around with anyone on the station. In his experience that was fraught with disaster. He'd been badly burnt before with a workplace romance on the mine and now he saved his romancing for other continents. He would prefer it if his crew played by the same rules but it wasn't something he could enforce, only suggest, and, let's face it, there often wasn't much else to do at the station, particularly over winter, and people got bored and fooled around.

He had been concerned about Sophie's perceived lack of experience but she'd proved herself today. It seemed she was going to be a good addition to the crew and he didn't want to jeopardise his position or hers by overstepping his self-imposed mark.

He didn't know why he was even thinking about it. Romance was probably the last thing on her mind. She had enough to deal with—she was in a foreign environment, she was exhausted and newly widowed—and it was unlikely she had the energy or desire for anything along the lines he was contemplating.

He needed to walk away.

He couldn't continue to stand there, watching her sleep. He couldn't get involved. He couldn't give in to temptation. It wasn't what either of them needed.

He was better off alone. He'd made that decision long ago and there was no reason to change his modus operandi now. He was the product of a broken home, of a father who'd lied and cheated and a mother who'd been unable to cope, and the one time he'd thought about risking everything for love he'd been spectacularly played for a fool. From then on he'd vowed never to get seriously involved in a relationship. Short-term flings, a weekend here and there, had become his way, and that worked for him. But it wouldn't work if he and Sophie were living under the same roof.

He didn't need complications.

Walk away, Gabe.

She doesn't need you to get involved. She doesn't need protecting. She's strong. She's made it here after everything she's been through. She doesn't need you.

Walk away.

Don't get involved.

Don't go looking for trouble.

He walked away.

CHAPTER FIVE

Date: March 9th
Temperature: -10°C
Hours of sunlight: 13.7

SOPHIE WOKE EARLY the next morning. She'd had an interrupted sleep, just the sound of Nikolai's breathing had been enough to disturb her. She hadn't realised she'd already grown used to the silence that came with sleeping alone.

Nikolai's condition was stable, she hadn't needed to stay in the clinic for the night but she'd been reluctant to leave him. She'd been worried his condition might deteriorate so it had been easier to stay, but she'd been surprised at how easily she'd fallen asleep. It had been the first night in a long time that she'd gone to sleep without thinking of Danny but she refused to feel guilty. That had been one reason for coming to Antarctica: she wanted to move forward. She didn't want to forget the past but she did want to put it behind her. She wanted to move on.

She closed her eyes and Gabe's soft, chocolate eyes came to mind. She could recall the easy feeling of confidence his smile gave her and the spark she'd felt when they'd touched. She'd wondered if that spark had just been adrenalin but she knew it was more than that. She was attracted to him, but was she exaggerating her reaction? Had the circumstances increased her awareness and response to him? Had the excitement of the day and her loneliness combined to make her hyper-aware? She wouldn't know until she saw him again. She wouldn't know the answer until she touched him again.

She kept one eye on the door, waiting for Gabe, but it was Finn who came to relieve her so she could shower and have breakfast. Gabe appeared only briefly later in the morning to get an update on Nikolai, but there was no reason to touch him and he seemed to be a little distant. Perhaps he had a lot on his mind but she felt silly. She must have been exaggerating the attraction, he certainly didn't seem to feel it.

Sophie attended to Nikolai and tried not to think about Gabe. The weather hadn't improved enough for Nikolai to be transferred so she would have a patient to keep her occupied for at least another twenty-four hours. She also needed to email Luke with the update she'd promised, but she didn't know where to start. How could she possibly be expected to describe her first day? She didn't think she could put yesterday's events into words. Only someone who had been through a similar experience would understand. Only someone who had been there would believe it. Someone like Gabe.

But no matter how much she tried to concentrate on other things, her mind kept returning to Gabe.

Was she betraying Danny with her thoughts?

She sighed. It was just something else to feel guilty about. Perhaps feeling guilty was something she was going to have to get used to. Unless she could block Gabe from her mind.

But she knew that was easier said than done. She had never had such a strong physical reaction to a man before. She'd always known that she and Danny were meant to be together but she didn't remember ever feeling such a strong sense that things were out of her control, that greater powers were at work. She and Danny had had a simple, straightforward relationship. She had no idea what sort of relationship she and Gabe were going to have but she had a feeling it wouldn't be simple. And until she had more time to try to work it out, she knew she needed to resist the pull of attraction.

Date: March 12th
Temperature: -8°C
Hours of sunlight: 13.3

Sophie was up with the sun. She was settling comfortably into station life and things were starting to become familiar. The weather had finally cleared and the Russians had collected Nikolai and Yuri's body, which meant she was free to leave the clinic and get out and have her first quad bike lesson with Alex. She was eager to get that ticked off because Gabe had promised to take her on an excursion once she had mastered the bike.

She had breakfast and dressed in all her layers and followed Alex outside. It was the first time she'd ventured from the red shed to one of the outbuildings and she was keen to get going, but Alex stopped her at the foot of the metal steps. He picked up a rope that was dangling from a metal pole and held it loosely in his hand. Sophie could trace the line of rope back to metal rings on the outer wall of the red shed.

'See these ropes?' he asked her. 'You'll find these between all the buildings. They're guide ropes. When the visibility is poor or in blizzard conditions these can be the only means you have of finding your way between the sheds. As long as you have hold of one of these, you can follow it from one building to the next.'

At various intervals between the red shed and the other sheds Sophie could see metal poles sticking out of the ice. Ropes were strung between the poles but she could see that they acted as guides, not barriers, as they hung low enough to rest on the ice and would allow vehicles to drive over them. It was a beautiful crisp, clear morning, much like the day she'd arrived, but now she understood just how quickly the weather could turn and she knew the guide ropes would have been invaluable in the whiteout conditions of her first full day.

She followed Alex along the line of the rope to the yellow machinery shed. It was massive and filled with an assortment of construction vehicles. Graders, trucks, forklifts, and snowmobiles were lined up inside, but Sophie was surprised to see quad bikes in the corner as well, and she realised she hadn't really imagined riding a four-wheeled motorbike over the snow.

'We're really using bikes? With wheels and tyres? We're not using the snowmobiles?' she asked.

'It's no different from driving the trucks that you see in here,' Alex said, and Sophie supposed that made sense. 'Quad bikes can be used on hard-packed snow and ice. Snowmobiles are for soft snow—powder snow. They're operated in the same way but because it's easier to tip a quad bike over I want to make sure you can handle that, but there are a few basics to understand before we can head out.'

Alex pulled a soft duffel bag from the back of a quad bike. 'Lesson one, protection. Wear the right clothing and take extra layers with you. Exposure to the weather kills more people than anything else. Always take a survival kit, you saw these the other day on our S&R. You need one between two people.' He opened the bag and proceeded to empty the contents, listing them off for Sophie's benefit as he unpacked and then repacked the kit.

'There's a tent and sleeping bags, spare clothing, a first-aid kit, spare radio, plus cooking equipment and rations for two days. *Always* make sure you've got one of these with you. You've seen how quickly the weather can change and once I've shown you how to use this equipment and set up the tent, this really can mean the difference between life and death.'

'Lesson two, communication. Always tell someone where you are going and when you expect to be back. Check in twice a day for overnight trips.' He showed her how to use the radio but this at least was familiar to her as she had used a similar system with the emergency retrieval team at the South Hobart Hospital.

'Lesson three, company. Never go out alone. That's one of Gabe's non-negotiable rules.'

'Does he have many?' she asked.

'Lots. But all for valid reasons.'

'He seems like a good leader.' Sophie couldn't resist trying to pump Alex for a little bit of information.

Alex nodded. 'He is. We have a strong team here and a lot of that is due to Gabe. It's a tough environment, unforgiving, and it presents a host of difficulties in terms of people management but Gabe handles it well. He has everyone's respect. We've become good mates over the past few years, as close as brothers in some ways. He's a great bloke but if you want to get out and about while you're here we need to forget about Gabe and make sure you're competent on a quad bike.'

'I'd better warn you, I'm a bit of a klutz.' Sophie was starting to feel a little nervous. She'd never ridden a motorbike before and now that she was standing here it was looking a little daunting.

'You can drive a car, can't you?'

'Yes, but I'm pretty well hopeless at anything that requires general co-ordination *and* balance. I don't need balance to drive a car but I'm not so sure about a quad bike.' There was a lot more to going out on a sightseeing trip in Antarctica than simply hopping into a car, but she knew that if she wanted to see anything of the icy continent she needed to pay attention and ensure she knew what to do.

'Have you ever ridden a motorbike?'

Sophie smiled and shook her head. 'I'm an emergency-room doctor. I've seen the damage people do to themselves on motorbikes.'

'Well, that's why it's important to understand the basics and the safety aspects. Can you ride a bicycle?'

'On flat ground.' She'd never been comfortable with off-road cycling because of her terrible balance and she hadn't ridden a bike since Danny's accident, and she didn't imagine she ever would again.

But this wasn't a bicycle. Balance, or lack of it, might not be such an issue and fortunately there didn't seem to be all that much that she could crash into out here. This was her adventure and she was determined to make the most of it.

She knew Danny would have loved this adventure, he would have been the first one to encourage her to have a go, but she was doing this for herself now, not for anyone else.

'We'll take it easy to begin with, Doc,' Alex promised, as he fitted her with a helmet and got her training under way.

Sophie lost track of time as she concentrated on following Alex's instructions and eventually he declared her competent. 'Now, would you like to take the lead and we can head back to the station?'

She looked around. They were out on the ice but she couldn't see the station and she knew of no landmarks. She'd lost track not only of time but also of direction. If she'd been on her own she would have been in dire straits. 'I have absolutely no idea where we are,' she admitted.

'All right, then, that means it's time for lesson four. Survival training. First step is planning—know where you plan to go, know how to use your GPS unit and have some basic navigational skills,' Alex said, and he proceeded to show her how the GPS unit worked. 'But you also need to have a back-up plan in case something does go wrong—there are several huts dotted at various distances from the station. It's important to know where the nearest hut is but, in a worst-case scenario, if you are injured or stranded away from any of the huts you need to know what to do in order to survive.'

He taught her how to set up a small bivouac tent, strung between their quad bikes and reinforced how important it was to have protection from the wind. 'Wind chill can be the killer in sub-zero temperatures. If you can get out of the wind you have a better chance of survival if it's twenty degrees below zero.'

'I have no intention of being out in those sorts of temperatures,' Sophie replied. She hoped she'd be cocooned inside the red shed if conditions were that atrocious.

'You were out in similar conditions on the search and rescue. Those conditions could have easily deteriorated and while I know you had plenty of experienced people with you we all have to be prepared for the worst, and to cope with the worst you need to be able to find food, shelter and warmth. And if you don't have shelter with you, you need to know how to build it.' He glanced at his watch and said, 'I think we have time for one final exercise before we should be heading back. Are you up for one last thing?'

Sophie had been on a steep learning curve. It had been another hectic day that had required lots of concentration but she found it exhilarating and the buzz meant she was far from tired. 'What is it?'

'I thought I'd show you how to make an ice cave.'

'Sure.'

Alex pulled some tools out of the survival kit and showed her how to dig a person-size depression in the snow, stopping after a couple of minutes to strip off his padded jacket. 'When you start to get warm you need to remove some clothing,' he told her. 'Don't allow sweat to gather inside your clothes, otherwise when you cool down again the moisture will make you cold.' Once he'd stripped down he showed her how to use a snow saw to cut blocks of ice that they laid across the hole for a ceiling.

'Why can't we just cut blocks of ice and build an igloo type structure on top of the ice?' Sophie asked. 'Why must we dig a hole first?'

'It keeps the wind out more effectively if we dig down first,' he replied. The cave was just about complete and Sophie was able to picture the finished version when they were interrupted by a radio call.

'Alex, this is Gabe, can you read me? Over.'

Alex looked at Sophie. 'You can take this one,' he said. 'See if you can remember what to do.'

Sophie picked up the handset for the two-way and depressed the 'talk' button.

'Gabe, this is Sophie. Over.'

'Doc, good. Listen, I need you back here. Dom's had an accident in the kitchen. He's sliced his finger quite badly. We can't stop the bleeding and I suspect it might need stitches. How far away are you? Over.'

Sophie turned to Alex. Despite the navigational training she really had no idea how far they were from the station, although she had a vague idea about in which direction it lay.

Alex took the handset from her and replied to Gabe. 'Twenty minutes. Over.'

'Okay. He's in the clinic. I'll meet you there. Over and out.'

Back at the station Sophie left Alex to put the quad bikes away and hurried into the red shed. She found Gabe and Dom in the clinic.

'Couldn't you find something else to use?' she asked, when she saw that Dom's left hand had been wrapped in a tea towel.

'It's a clean one,' Dom quipped.

'It's also the third one we've used and the cut is still bleeding,' Gabe added, as Sophie washed her hands and pulled on a pair of surgical gloves. Gabe's tone was calm and measured but Sophie heard the unspoken message that, despite Dom's jokes, the injury wasn't a minor one. Gabe had told Sophie that he thought the cut needed stitching and Sophie trusted his judgement.

'Which finger is it?' she asked, as she nodded in response to Gabe's comments.

'Index.'

She unwrapped Dom's bloodied hand, keeping some pressure on his index finger. Amongst the dried blood she could see several old scars, which she assumed were from previous knife cuts, and he was missing the very tip of his middle finger too. Carefully she exposed the latest injury, relieved to find that, although the cut was deep and would need stitching, the edges were at least clean and smooth. Dom had obviously been using a sharp knife.

'I will need to stitch this but it's not too difficult,' she said, as she administered a ring block anaesthetic. She didn't want him wriggling while she was trying to stitch the wound. While she waited for the anaesthetic to kick in she got a suturing kit out of the cupboard and opened it up.

'What were you cutting?' she asked, as she checked Dom's finger to see if the anaesthetic had taken effect.

'Carrots for the roast and the knife slipped.'

'Can you feel that?' she asked as she pricked the end of his finger.

Dom shook his head and Sophie threaded the needle and began stitching.

'Can I have a waterproof dressing over that, Doc?' he asked as Gabe snipped the thread for her. 'I need to finish off dinner prep.'

'You're not going back into the kitchen,' she said. 'You've got the rest of the day off. If you keep working, it's likely to keep bleeding. There must be someone else who can chop a few carrots. I can do it if necessary,' she offered.

'I'll take care of the prep,' Gabe told Dom. 'We'll see you in time for the meal.'

Dom was sent to his donga to rest and Sophie followed Gabe to the kitchen. A mountain of vegetables was piled onto the stainless-steel island. Dom didn't appear to have got very far into the pile before tragedy had struck. Sophie sat at the bench and watched Gabe chop and slice his way through the mound. There was no reason for her to stay but she was reluctant to go. She had nothing else she had to do and sitting enjoying his company was preferable to spending time alone in her room.

'How did you go with Alex?' he asked her.

'Good. He said he'll sign me off as competent on a quad bike so now I can go exploring.'

'Not alone, though.' Gabe's brown eyes were serious as he paused in his slicing and dicing to look at her.

'Don't worry, I know. I've had a thorough safety briefing too. But I would like to get out and have a look around,' she said, picking up a vegetable peeler and a potato and starting to peel. They had the kitchen to themselves and if she was going to sit there chatting she might as well work. If she didn't help, she suspected dinner would run very late.

'I'll see what I can do,' Gabe replied. 'We have Sundays off and people usually go somewhere then, weather permitting.'

'Where do they go?'

'There's a penguin colony not far from here, that's where we take most of our new expeditioners for their first trip. The quintessential Antarctic experience.' He smiled at her and Sophie felt a rush of heat through her bones. 'Sometimes a group will go off cross-country skiing or out to one of the huts just for a change of scenery.'

'What do you like to do in your spare time?'

'I don't seem to have a lot of that but I enjoy dusting off the cross-country skis in good weather and I like to potter around in the kitchen too.'

'Do you miss being a chef?'

'Not really. If I want to cook, Dom's always happy to lend me his kitchen.'

'What made you become a chef? Was your mum a good cook or did your family have a restaurant?'

'Why would you think that?'

'People seem to gravitate to what they've been exposed to.'

'So you come from a line of medicos?'

'No.' Sophie smiled. 'I grew up on a farm of sorts. My parents had an apple and pear orchard south of Hobart.'

'Had?'

'They're retired now. They sold the property and moved to Queensland.'

'But you ended up a doctor.'

'It was either that or a vet. When I was at school I always had an animal hospital, and any injured wildlife I found on the property I'd care for. Possums, sugar gliders, the occasional joey. But by the time I had almost finished school I'd decided to study medicine. My grandpa was a doctor so I guess I followed in his footsteps. The orchard was his hobby but my father's passion so I guess the medical gene just skipped a generation. I always wanted to fix animals and people. I still do.' But she hadn't been able to fix Danny. She pushed that thought aside as she finished peeling the last potato and it wasn't until much later that she realised Gabe hadn't answered her question. He hadn't told her why he'd become a chef or what had made him change careers.

Dinner had been cleared away, Dom had retired to his room and Gabe was pretending to read but in reality he was watching Sophie. Alex had challenged her to a game of Scrabble, which was interesting in itself, Gabe had never known him to have an interest in board games, but it wasn't the fact that Alex was playing Scrabble that was fascinating Gabe, it was Sophie. The new doc had really knocked him for a six. He hadn't expected her. He'd expected someone less capable, less attractive and less desirable.

He'd missed her today when she'd been away from the red shed. That in itself was ridiculous. How could he miss someone he barely knew? But already he was used to having her around, already he noticed a hole in his day when she wasn't there to fill it.

He knew he needed to keep his distance in order to keep some perspective.

He laughed to himself. What he really needed was to get laid. It had been too long between women. Maybe that would sort him out. The trouble was it was going to be several more months before he would be back in Australia. It would be several months before he would be able to scratch that itch.

So that meant more cold showers for him but, of course, he had to be living where there were water restrictions. Everything was conspiring against him.

He had deliberately avoided relationships since coming to Antarctica. His last serious relationship had ended three years ago, imploding spectacularly and precipitating his move to the ice. He'd had enough of women and Antarctica had seemed like a pretty good place to go if he wanted to avoid them. He saved his romancing for his leave, a weekend here and there, which meant he was able to avoid anything that could resemble a relationship and, to date, it had been relatively easy. In three years he hadn't met anyone who had tempted him. Until now. Until Sophie.

But if Alex was keen on Sophie too that presented a different problem. Over the past three years he and Alex had formed a strong friendship and, if anyone had asked, Gabe would have said Alex was like a brother to him. But that didn't give him the right to ask what his intentions were or to ask him to back off. Alex knew Gabe's thoughts on relationships and Gabe suspected he would give Gabe his blessing if he knew that Sophie had caught his eye but that wasn't the point.

Sophie was out of bounds. It didn't matter that since she'd arrived on the scene he hadn't been able to stop thinking about her. She had captivated his attention, crept unbidden into his thoughts and interrupted his concentration and made him contemplate breaking his self-imposed rule.

But he knew he was being ridiculous. He knew he had to walk away.

He'd only known her for five days. Surely he could resist her.

Walk away, Gabe.

She wasn't worth risking his heart for. It would only be asking for trouble. At least, that's what he tried to tell himself but every time Sophie smiled and her dimples flashed his resolve was sorely tested.

Toughen up, he told himself, *she's just a woman. There are dozens just like her.*

But as he walked away he wasn't sure that was true.

CHAPTER SIX

Date: March 15th
Temperature: -12°C
Hours of sunlight: 13.0

THE WEATHER HAD closed in again but Sophie didn't mind being cooped up inside. She'd had a couple of outdoor experiences and, while one had been far more relaxed than the other, both had left her exhausted. It was hard work, being outside in this climate. The conditions were much harsher than she'd anticipated and it required a lot of concentration to stay focussed. Indoor tasks were far more familiar to her and came much more naturally. She felt as though she had things under control while she was inside.

She'd been busy for the past couple of days, so busy that she'd even had a day when she hadn't thought about Danny, but she'd refused to feel guilty about it, which made a pleasant change. Maybe coming to the ice would be the cure she was hoping for. Maybe she would be okay.

Along with routine medical care she also needed to schedule a series of health screenings for a few of the crazier expeditioners who were planning on taking part in an outdoor swim—the annual April Fools' Day swim. Sophie couldn't understand what the attraction was in stripping down to a pair of swimmers and jumping into water that was near freezing, neither could she believe that this activity was actually on the station calendar and sanctioned by the AAP, but part of her role in occupational heath and safety meant she had to do health checks on anyone who was planning to participate.

The health checks were relatively straightforward and required her to check general fitness and heart function. There were a dozen expeditioners who had signed up, all men, not surprisingly—women had more sense—and Sophie needed to get started on their checks. Some had made an appointment to see her, others, including Gabe, hadn't as yet.

She sent a reminder email to those who hadn't booked in. To Gabe's she added a note that she'd heard from Dr John, hoping that would encourage him to come and see her. She'd been too busy to think about Danny but not too busy to notice that she hadn't crossed paths with Gabe for a day or two and she'd missed his company. She hadn't yet got to know many people, the crew on the station were busy with their own jobs and her role was relatively independent, broken only by brief periods when she needed to see a patient, but there was no one on her team as such. Alex, Dom, Finn and Gabe were the only ones she'd formed any sort of connection with and she felt most comfortable with Gabe. She liked him and she liked the way he made her feel. Just seeing him could make her smile. He made her feel happy.

Her email worked. Within half an hour Gabe stuck his head into the clinic.

'Hey, Doc.' His greeting was relaxed, no explanation as to why he was there or whether he'd even seen her email.

'Hi. Have you come for your medical check?' Sophie tried to remain calm and collected too but her spirits lifted the moment he smiled at her and her immediate reaction was one of excitement.

'No, I thought you'd be busy. I just wanted to catch up with Doc John's news about his daughter.'

'Did he email you as well?'

'He did but there was a bit of medical jargon in there that didn't make a lot of sense. I thought you could explain what it meant. If you've got time?'

'Sure.' Sophie opened John's email on her computer, thinking she'd focus better if she looked at the screen instead of at Gabe, but his next move distracted her even further. He wheeled a small stool over and sat behind her, looking over her shoulder. She could feel his breath on her neck, little puffs of warm air that made her spine tingle and made the soft hair at the base of her skull stand on end.

She was terribly conscious that he sat just inches behind her. She sat a bit straighter in her chair, trying to put some space between them so she could concentrate, but it took a lot of effort.

'Okay. Marianna's tumour is benign, which is good news. It means it won't spread into other areas of her body but it is quite large and until the surgeons operate they don't really know if they'll be able to get it all out. The question is whether they will be able to excise all of it without doing other damage.'

'If it's benign, does it have to come out?'

'Yes. If they leave it, it will continue to grow and that's not what they want, but surgery itself is a risk. There's always the chance that Marianna won't make it through, which is why John wanted the surgeons to wait until he got home before they operated. In case she doesn't make it.'

'I thought his tone was quite positive in the email he sent me.'

'There's certainly more good news than bad at this

stage, but I think he's keen to have some time at home to support both his wife and daughter while Marianna recovers.'

'The supply ship will leave Hobart around the end of March to make its final trip down here before winter,' Gabe said, 'so he has another couple of weeks to see how things play out before he needs to decide whether or not to get on the ship to come back down here.'

In two weeks she would know if John was returning. She would know if her time here would be short-lived. It was going so fast already. There was so much she wanted to experience, what if she didn't get a chance? She wanted to make the most of every opportunity and that included spending more time with Gabe. To delay him, she decided to ask about the logistics of the swim.

'Have you got time to explain the April Fools' Day swim to me?'

'Sure. What would you like to know?'

'I need to know what the routine is. What's expected of me?'

'Liam and Duncan will dig a pool down by the harbour and they usually get it ready a week or so beforehand so you'll be able to have a look at it in advance. The ice will be at least a metre thick and they'll use the excavator to rip through it to make the pool. The pool is smallish, not that the dimensions matter to you but it'll be a couple of metres wide by about four long. Just big enough to get wet in.'

'What is the water temperature?

'At this time of year it'll be between zero and two degrees Celsius.'

'That's freezing!'

'Not quite. Sea water here freezes at about minus two degrees. Don't worry,' he said with a grin, 'no one stays in for long but for the swim to count they have to put their heads under water. But before we go ahead the conditions have to be right in terms of wind speed. A sunny day with little or, better yet, no wind is ideal.'

'How do people get warm again afterwards?'

'Space blankets and fleece-lined boots,' Gabe told her. 'We set up a small hut next to the pool with a heater. It becomes like a little sauna and everyone hops in there after their dip to dry off and get dressed but there's also a tradition of defrosting in a warm spa later. It gets fired up on special occasions.'

'Has anyone ever had a medical emergency?' Sophie knew the shock of jumping into an icy-cold pool could be enough to trigger cardiac arrest in some cases.

'No, but John did take the defibrillator with him last year.'

'Great, that's reassuring.'

'Better to be safe than sorry.'

'Better not to do the swim at all, I would have thought,' Sophie retorted, and Gabe laughed. She was glad she was needed on standby and therefore not under any pressure to join in the swim.

'Where would the fun be in that?'

'It sounds like you're still planning on joining in?'

'I am.'

She raised an eyebrow. 'So shall I do your check-up now then?'

'No, I can wait. I've taken up enough of your day.'

'I've got time and I'm guessing you do too. You seem to have plenty of time to chat so let's get it out of the way.'

Gabe shrugged and gave in. 'All right, you're the boss. Where would you like me?'

'Take your shirt off and have a seat on the bed,' she said, as she turned to pull his file out of the cabinet. When she turned back she found he had done as she'd asked and was sitting on the bed, bare-chested.

She was staring straight at his broad shoulders and tanned chest. His pectoral muscles were lightly covered with dark hair that trailed down to his navel, dividing a toned six-pack and leading her eyes lower. She hadn't really thought this through. She was an experienced doctor, and so was used to seeing naked or semi-naked men, but for some reason the sight of Gabe sitting bare-chested in front of her set her pulse racing. He was very male and his hard, solid body threw her into a state of confusion.

Danny had been muscular but lean and wiry and what little chest hair he'd had had been fair. Gabe was such a contrast to what Sophie was used to and seeing him in all his glory was really confusing her. Her memories of Danny were becoming jumbled and that unsettled her.

She swallowed and tried to think of something to say that sounded professional. After all, it was just a routine physical examination. If she could just remember that.

'Any medical history that I should be aware of?'

Gabe shook his head.

'No family history of high blood pressure or cardiac problems?' she asked, as she opened out the automatic blood-pressure cuff. And that presented her with another dilemma. She hadn't thought about having to touch him. The feel of his bare skin under her fingers as she wrapped the sphygmomanometer cuff around his arm set her nerves on fire and she had to focus hard to stop her hands from shaking.

Her reaction reminded her of the first time she'd had to examine a cute, nearly naked twenty-something man when she'd been a med student. She'd blushed and stammered her way through the exam then too. But she wasn't a med student any longer, she was an experienced doctor, and she should be able to examine a man without losing her cool or her concentration.

She wasn't a student and Gabe was definitely not a twenty-year-old youth. He was all man. There was no disputing that. She needed to focus.

She was a professional. She needed to act like one.

She turned away while the blood-pressure cuff inflated. She picked up a stethoscope. She didn't need it to take his blood pressure, the machine would do that automatically, but she would need it to listen to his chest, and it gave her a reason to step away, gave her something to do while she got her hormones under control.

The machine beeped at her and she returned to Gabe's side. 'BP and pulse normal,' she told him as she switched off the machine and unwrapped the cuff.

She placed the bulb of the stethoscope onto his chest. His pecs were well defined, his chest was solid and his stomach was flat with ridges of abdominals. His physique was undoubtedly masculine but she tried to convince herself he was just another patient as she ran her eyes over his smooth, olive skin.

'Deep breaths, in and out through your nose for me,' she said, as she moved the stethoscope around and tried to ignore the fluttering in her stomach.

She bent her head as she listened to his breathing and she could feel each one of his exhalations as a soft puff of air on her cheek. She closed her eyes and found herself breathing in time with him.

When she lifted her head and opened her eyes as she finished listening she found herself staring into his chocolate-brown gaze. Their lips were millimetres apart. If she tipped her chin just the slightest fraction she would be able to taste him. She held herself still, terrified that if she moved she wouldn't be able to resist pressing her lips to his.

She held herself rigid as Gabe lifted his hands and plucked the stethoscope from her ears. His hands brushed her cheeks and Sophie held her breath as he looped the stethoscope around her neck.

He leaned towards her. Was he going to kiss her? There could only be a space the width of a butterfly wing between their lips and she swore it must be one of the butterflies that had escaped from her belly.

She knew he was about to kiss her but at the very last moment she chickened out, turning her head and stepping away. She couldn't do this. She didn't know how.

She'd never let a man take control like this. Without uttering a word, she could feel him pulling her in. Seducing her. But she didn't know how to let go. She didn't know how to let herself be seduced.

She had lost her virginity to Danny but they had been friends first. There had been nothing uncomfortable about it but there had also been no seduction. For she and Danny it had just been the next logical step and that was how it had felt. That first time had been good but hadn't set her world on fire or her heart alight, but somehow she knew that getting to close to Gabe would be different. Getting close to Gabe would be flirting with danger, playing with fire, and she would most likely get burnt.

She had no experience in this adult game of lust and desire. She'd been safe with Danny but Gabe felt dangerous. While she felt she could trust him to keep her from any physical danger, matters of the flesh were a different story.

She stepped back on shaky legs and her hands shook too as she picked up a heart-rate monitor and tried to ignore what had just passed between them.

'Time for your fitness test,' she said, and her voice

wavered and wobbled as nervousness combined with breathlessness.

She handed him the monitor. He'd have to strap it around his own chest, she wasn't game. She needed some distance, some time to gather her thoughts, and doing the fitness test now would buy her some valuable time.

'So, how'd I do?' he asked without a trace of breathlessness as she slowed the treadmill down after ten minutes.

Her heart rate had recovered while Gabe had walked on the treadmill but she suspected it would still be beating faster than his. 'Unfortunately, you're as fit as a fiddle.' If she'd been able to fail him he wouldn't have been able to take part in the swim, a result she would have been happy with.

'I'm good to go, then?'

'I guess so but that doesn't mean I condone this exercise. I'd like it on record that I think it's a stupid idea.'

'I can't say I disagree with you, Doc.'

'Then why on earth are you planning on going ahead with this?'

'It's a tradition and, as station leader, I feel I need to take part. These types of activities, while possibly stupid, are good for team bonding and morale. The sort of thing that men need to take part in, especially when we're down here for months on end with only a few people, it's important to foster team spirit.'

'But what about the safety aspect? Don't you think it's important to be mindful of that?'

'That's why it's compulsory to have these health checks first. Alex will take care of the logistics of the exercise and he takes his responsibilities very seriously. Provided he and I think the activity is safe on the day in terms of the weather conditions, the site and everyone's physical fitness, we'll consider it a low-risk activity and I'm prepared to put my hand up and join in. They're my team and I like to lead from the front.'

That fitted perfectly with what she'd surmised about Gabe's personality so far. He was someone who would have your back, someone strong and dependable. She'd seen how he treated everyone with respect and the respect they gave him in return. He was just the sort of man you'd want to have on your team.

'You'll get the final say on the day,' he reassured her. 'You'll get a chance to double-check our BPs, heart rates and anything else you want before we jump in. You'll have to trust Alex and me to take care of the rest. Deal?'

His dark brown eyes locked onto hers. He was so calm and convincing. So dependable. Everyone else at the station seemed to trust him implicitly and from everything she had seen so far she had no reason to doubt his word. Until she had reason to think otherwise, she would continue to trust him too.

She stuck out her hand. 'Deal.'

Gabe took her hand in his and as his fingers wrapped around hers she knew she could trust him, she just wasn't sure she could trust herself.

CHAPTER SEVEN

Date: March 17th
Temperature: -11°C
Hours of sunlight: 12.7

SOPHIE HID IN the clinic for the next two days, using her diary as a shield. She had appointments booked solid. Not only did she have to see the expeditioners who were planning on joining in the April Fools' Day swim but many were due for their regular bimonthly health checks as well. In order to get through all the appointments, she offered to see expeditioners in their lunchtime, giving her a reason to take a late or early lunch and therefore avoid Gabe.

She was finding it difficult to get the image of a semi-naked Gabe out of her head, and their almost-kiss, and she was worried about behaving normally around him. Her plan was to avoid him for a few days in the hope that the picture would fade and she'd be back to normal. Then she might be able to trust herself not to embarrass either of them.

She managed to fill her spare time too, either by reading or by hiding in the hydroponics shed, where she'd volunteered her time, but there was no escaping Saturday-night activities. Psychologists who had made a career of studying people who were subjected to long periods of working in isolation, including at Antarctic stations, had recommended a weekly activity as a way of breaking up the routine, or sometimes the monotony, of life on the ice. This was particularly important over the winter season when the expeditioners couldn't necessarily get outside. The Saturday-night festivities gave them all something to look forward to and a reason to socialise, and Sophie knew she'd be expected to join in.

One thing she was looking forward to after ten days on the ice was dressing in something a bit smarter than a T-shirt and leggings or scrubs. A couple of women who had worked on the ice before her had suggested that she pack a couple of skirts or dresses to be worn on Saturday nights. Everyone made a bit more of an effort, again mostly to break the monotony and differentiate the weekend from the rest of the week, but it felt good to bathe and wash her hair with a purpose in mind, rather than just because it was her turn to have a shower.

Carey station always tried to find something to celebrate on a Saturday night and this Saturday was tailor made for a celebration—it was St Patrick's Day.

Sophie dressed in a soft, emerald-green silk dress. Sleeveless with a belted waist and a skirt that fell in narrow pleats, it was one of her favourites. It made her eyes look exceptionally green and always made her feel confident. It had seemed a luxury when she'd packed it but it had rolled up so small that she'd convinced herself she had room for it and she was glad she'd brought it. She left her hair loose and it fell in thick, dark waves past her shoulders. She brushed some green eye shadow over her lids and moistened her lips with a pale pink gloss as she tried to ignore the thought that she might be dressing for Gabe.

The dining room had been decorated and Dom, who after agreeing to take one day off after his incident with the knife, was back in the kitchen, cooking up an Irish feast, which meant lots of potatoes and lamb and Guinness. Irish flags decorated the walls and someone had cut enormous four-leaf clovers out of green plastic and decorated the tables.

Everyone was expected to wear something green and everyone appeared to have made an extra effort with their outfits. Alex had a gigantic green top hat perched on his blond curls and Finn looked dapper in a green velvet smoking jacket. Where that had come from and why he'd have it in Antarctica Sophie vowed to find out, until she was distracted by Gabe and forgot all about Finn.

He was wearing snug denim jeans with a rich green polo shirt that hugged his chest and arms. He wasn't dressed up as elaborately as some of the others but he looked gorgeous. The shirt made the most of his toned physique and she could picture exactly what was underneath it. It had seemed ridiculous to pack a dress but she was glad now that she had. Gabe looked fantastic and suddenly Sophie wanted to look her best too.

Dinner was self-service and as Sophie picked up a plate and stood in line, Gabe stepped in behind her.

'Happy St Paddy's Day, Doc,' he greeted her as he reached past to grab a plate. He seemed calm and relaxed as usual and it was probably just coincidence that he was beside her but her senses were heightened. He smelt fresh and clean and Sophie had a sudden urge to lean a little closer to fully appreciate his scent.

'What category have you nominated for in the Annual Paddy's darts and pool competition?' he asked, as the line moved slowly forwards.

'Category?'

'We have a darts and billiards competition as part of

the night's festivities. The sign-up sheet has been on the notice-board for a couple of days. Haven't you seen it?'

Sophie shook her head. 'It doesn't sound like my kind of thing.'

'Everyone is expected to nominate for one or the other,' he told her. 'Finn is the current darts champion and Alex is the pool champ. Challengers play against each other to win the right to challenge the champion.'

'I can't imagine doing either. I'm hopeless at all sports.'

'You have to put your name down for something. This is what's at stake.' At the end of one of the tables were two huge trophies, which had been engraved with the names of past champions around their bases. 'So, which will it be?'

'It will have to be pool, not darts,' she told him. 'You definitely don't want to be around if I'm throwing sharp, pointy things.'

Gabe laughed and steered her past the notice-board and waited while she added her name to the list.

The competition got under way as soon as dinner was finished. The Guinness was flowing, along with plenty of red wine, and it didn't take much encouragement from the crowd to convince Liam to get his violin out and play some music to accompany the games. Liam played the violin like a fiddle and a couple of the scientists gave a reasonable demonstration of some Irish dancing as Sophie waited for her turn at the pool table.

Her opponent was Andrew, an engineer. 'Would you like to rack or break?' he asked.

'I have no idea what you're talking about.'

'Racking is just what we call it when you set the balls up at the beginning of the game, using this.' Andrew was holding a plastic triangle in his hand. 'Breaking just means having the first shot to break up the rack. If I rack, you'll break,' he explained.

That didn't make things any clearer for her but as she didn't know if there was a right and wrong way to rack the balls but thought she could probably manage to hit one if they were all grouped together, she replied, 'I think I'll break.'

Watching him rack the balls and chalk his cue, she suspected he'd done this before. She had never played and as she wondered what she'd got herself into, Gabe arrived at her side. 'Do you think I should just forfeit now and get it over with?' she asked him.

'I didn't think you'd be the type to roll over quite so easily.'

He was right. It wasn't in her nature to give up at the first hurdle. 'I'm not,' she agreed, before asking, 'So which stick do I use, then?'

'It's called a "cue",' Gabe explained as he selected one for her and rubbed a small chalk block over the end, just as Andrew had done.

'What's that for?'

'It stops the cue from slipping off the ball,' he replied as he handed her the stick.

Sophie reached for the cue, taking it before Gabe had released it. Her hand closed over the top of his and a surge of adrenalin ran through her. She could feel her hand shake and wondered how she would ever be able to hit the ball now. She swallowed hard and tried to ignore the heat that was pooling in her belly. All she could see in her mind's eye was the image of semi-naked Gabe, stripped down to his waist, bare-chested and sitting in her clinic. She stepped back and tried to focus on the green of his shirt instead of thinking back to the last image she had of him when he'd been semi-naked and about to kiss her. She turned away and tried to focus on the green felt of the pool table and concentrate on the game.

She rested her left hand on the surface of the table, like she thought she'd seen others do, and standing upright she tried to line up a shot.

'Here, do it like this.' Having relinquished the cue, Gabe was now standing behind her. 'Lean over the table and put your left hand like this.' He demonstrated the position and Sophie did as instructed, only to find that he was leaning over her shoulder and readjusting her position. 'Look down the line of the cue and take aim.'

Gabe's left arm was stretched out alongside hers. His right arm wrapped around her back and guided her hand on the cue. She tried to ignore the fact that her bottom was pressed into Gabe's groin but her silk dress was so flimsy she could feel his body heat pulsing through the thin fabric.

Once Gabe seemed confident that she had the correct stance, he stepped back. Sophie let out her breath, closed her eyes and hoped for the best. Somehow she managed to connect with the white ball and sent it crashing into the coloured balls, scattering them across the table.

'Not bad, Doc,' Gabe said.

Andrew took his shot and Sophie watched as a coloured ball fell into a corner pocket. She was wondering what she should do for her turn when Andrew lined up for a second shot.

'Isn't it my turn?' she asked Gabe.

'Not until Andrew misses,' he replied. 'If you pot a ball, you get another turn.'

Andrew's next shot missed the pocket so Sophie started to line up. The black ball looked as if it was in a good spot but Gabe stopped her. 'Stay away from the black ball.'

'Why?'

'That's the money ball but you can't sink it until you've got all your other ones in. You're smalls,' he said.

'I'm what?' She felt as though Gabe and Andrew were

speaking a foreign language. None of this made any sense. No wonder she hated sports.

'You have to try to sink the seven solid colour balls, the ones with the low numbers. If you hit one of Andrew's first or sink one of his by mistake he'll get an extra shot. If you sink the black one before all your others, Andrew wins. Aim for the yellow one.' Sophie lined the shot up but Gabe obviously thought she could do better. He leaned over her right shoulder and wrapped his arms around her as he corrected the angle of her shot, and Sophie thought she'd perhaps been too hasty in her dislike of all sports. She might learn to enjoy pool. 'Don't hit it too hard, just try to push it down the table towards the back pocket.'

Somehow she managed to pull off the shot and the yellow ball tumbled into the pocket. 'Good work!' Gabe said, and he high-fived her, but her new-found enjoyment of the game slowly dissipated as the rest of her balls languished on the table while Andrew sank three more.

'I don't think this is my game.'

'Don't worry. Andrew's clearing the table. It'll make it easier for you.' Gabe laughed.

Andrew had sunk five of his balls before Sophie got another one in. In a burst of excitement and delight she threw her arms around Gabe's neck and hugged him. He lifted her off her feet. 'Well done. I knew you'd get the hang of this.'

But that was the end of her success. Once Gabe released her she couldn't focus at all. Having Gabe's arms around her had put her into a spin. She felt giddy and off balance but in a good way. She felt excited and desirable. Alive.

The spark wasn't adrenalin. It wasn't circumstances or her imagination. There was most definitely chemistry. But while it made her feel good, she didn't think she could, or should, do anything about it. She wasn't ready for that.

She missed everything from that point on and Andrew wasted no time in finishing off the game. She stayed to watch Gabe as he challenged Andrew next. He wasn't doing any better than she had—well, he did sink more balls but still not enough to win—but she was only vaguely aware of how he'd done as she'd been completely distracted by the sight of his bum in his jeans as he'd leant over the table. She occasionally remembered to watch Andrew or turn her attention to the darts contest but her eye was constantly returning to Gabe.

She was lonely, she knew it, and while she didn't plan on being alone for the rest of her life, that was different than mistaking loneliness for attraction. She didn't want to make a mistake just because she was lonely.

In the background she was aware of Liam's music continuing. She recognised the opening notes of 'Danny Boy' and then Dom joined in with the lyrics.

This had been their song, hers and Danny's, and she hadn't listened to it in seven months.

She'd always loved this song, she'd used to sing it to Danny but now she found the haunting, lilting strains sorrowful as memories of Danny flooded back to her. She knew she wouldn't be able to listen to this song now without crying, and she definitely didn't want to cry in front of everyone. She escaped to her room, leaving Gabe and Andrew to finish their game.

Back in her donga Sophie rebooted her laptop. She needed to see Danny's face. Thinking about Danny made her feel guilty for the attraction she felt towards Gabe because if she closed her eyes right now it wasn't Danny's face she saw. Semi-naked, smiling Gabe was still the vision that sprang to mind. She'd had that image in her head for the past couple of days and bending over the pool table with

Gabe's arms around her was doing nothing to tone it down. She needed to see Danny. To reconnect.

Before the computer could come to life there was a knock on her door. Sophie glanced in the mirror. She looked a mess. Her eyes were watery and her nose was red. She quickly blew her nose before opening the door.

Gabe stood in front of her. 'You all right, Doc?'

Perhaps she looked worse than she'd thought. She wasn't all right but she nodded anyway and started to make excuses. 'I'm not normally such a basket case but that song reminded me of Danny.'

'Your husband?'

She nodded and stepped back, giving Gabe space to enter her room. She didn't want to talk about Danny while standing in the doorway. Did she want to talk about him at all?

Her donga, all the dongas, were small and she was very aware of Gabe and how much room he filled. She sat cross-legged at the head of her bed to give herself some breathing space. Gabe sat at the opposite end. There wasn't anywhere for him *to* sit other than the small chair at her desk and she had clothes draped all over that.

'Are you sure you're okay?' he asked again.

She shook her head. 'I'm fine. Just every now and then something will catch me unawares. I just felt a little bit sad.'

'Is that Danny?'

Her laptop had finally decided to wake up and her screensaver showed the photo of Danny. He was watching them with his goofy smile on his face.

Sophie didn't want him watching them. She didn't want him to watch Gabe sitting on her bed. She reached out and closed the lid.

'Do you want to talk about him?'

'Why?'

'If you're missing him, it might be nice to have someone to talk to about him. Why don't you tell me something? How did you meet?'

Perhaps it would help to talk about him. Perhaps it would make his memory clearer. Maybe it would lessen her guilt.

Was she finally healing or was she forgetting?

She wasn't sure but wasn't this what she'd wanted? A chance to start over? Could she do this? Could she talk about Danny to the only other man who took her breath away?

She met Gabe's brown gaze and prepared to give it a go.

'I'd known Danny practically all my life. We met on the first day of high school when we were assigned each other as lab partners in science class. Danny wanted to test the boundaries even back then and I had to rein him in to stop him from blowing us all to smithereens. That set the pattern for our relationship right from the start. He was always on the go, experimenting, trying different things, I was always the conservative one who followed the rules, but he did encourage me to test my own limits.

'I don't really remember not knowing him. I don't re-member what I was like before I met him and that's why it's been so hard to find myself now that he's gone. So much of me is tied up with Danny and I'm not really sure who I am without him.

'He was so fearless. He never doubted himself. He never thought there was something he couldn't do and he made me feel the same way. He gave me the confidence to test myself.'

That was something she'd noticed in Gabe too. Both men seemed to have the ability to bolster her self-confi-dence. On a couple of occasions when she'd been nervous or out of her depth all Gabe had needed to do had been look at her with his dark brown eyes and she'd instantly felt more capable. But she was talking about Danny now.

'He gave me confidence and I kept him safe. Until one day I couldn't.'

'You couldn't? I thought he died in a road accident.'

Gabe's comment surprised her. She hadn't realised he would be privy to that information.

'It's a note in your file,' he explained apologetically.

'He was bike riding when a reckless driver crashed into him, but if I hadn't taken an extra shift at work to cover for someone who called in sick he would have been home with me. He would have been safe. But instead our lives were changed in an instant.'

'It wasn't your fault.'

'Wasn't it?' She still grappled with the guilt and she thought she might always feel that way. She didn't know how to get past that feeling.

'Is that when you applied to come here? After he died?'

She nodded. 'I'd been working at the AMU for a while but hadn't thought about actually coming to Antarctica until Danny was killed. Danny had sparked my sense of adventure and I decided that coming to the ice would be a good goal to focus on. Getting here gave me something to strive for, a reason to keep going. Because of Dr John's situation it all happened a bit faster than I expected but I have no regrets. It's what I wanted to do, it's where I want to be.

'Back in Hobart every day someone would ask how I was doing. People seemed to expect me not to cope. It was like I was expected to be in a permanent state of grief. It wasn't healthy. It felt like I wasn't allowed to get on with my life. It made me feel guilty for wanting to move on and that was on top of the guilt I already felt over the accident. I needed to get away and when the opportunity came up to relieve John down here I jumped at it. It was my chance to leave my old life for a while, a chance to start afresh. I wanted to be where people didn't know about my history. Being here is about me starting over again.'

Gabe was smiling and immediately Sophie could feel her sadness lifting. 'That's why most people come here,' he said. 'To get away from everyday life. Antarctica is the last frontier. We're like the Australian explorers in the eighteen hundreds or the American pioneers. But a lot of us bring our problems with us. It's not easy to run away completely.'

'I'm not running away but I can't stay in the past. Life goes on. Danny would be the first person to tell me that I need to keep living. I thought coming here would give me a chance to move on. I thought that by being somewhere where no one knew me as one half of Danny and Sophie I would cope better. I didn't expect to have reminders of Danny here. I don't want to forget about him but I can't live the rest of my life mourning him.'

'You're willing to have another go?'

'At love?'

Gabe nodded.

'Yes. I don't believe there's only one person for every-body. I know there's not. I'd planned to spend the rest of my life with Danny and that isn't how things have turned out, but I don't believe that's it for me. I refuse to believe it. I'm thirty-one, I don't want to be on my own for the rest of my life. I came here to learn how to be on my own again but I don't want to be on my own for ever.' She shrugged. 'I have to hope love comes along again one day. Do you see things differently? Do you think people have one soul mate and one only?'

'I have no idea how it works.'

'Have you ever been in love?' she asked.

'Not very successfully.'

'What does that mean?'

'It means I'm better off alone.'

'No one is better off alone,' she argued. 'Not for ever.'

'I am.'

'Gee, someone really did a number on you.' She wondered what his story was. 'Were you married?'

'No.' Gabe was shaking his head. 'But she was.'

'She was married? And you didn't know?'

'Of course not.'

'Ouch.' Sophie didn't know if Gabe was deliberately trying to distract her by redirecting the conversation but he was doing a pretty good job. Her curiosity was piqued. 'When was this?'

'A long time ago.'

'And you've been on your own ever since?'

'No man is an island,' he replied with a grin, 'but I have avoided anything serious since then and I've found I'm quite happy with the alternative.'

'Don't you get lonely? Don't you want to find your other half? The person who really understands you and knows you intimately and loves you anyway?'

'I don't believe in all that. Exposing yourself to another person like that makes you vulnerable. You open yourself up to a world of pain.'

'What exactly did this woman do to you!? What happened that made you so pessimistic about true love?'

'Apart from lying about her marital status, you mean?'

'Apart from that.' Sophie smiled. 'I get why you might take umbrage at being lied to but you can't tar all women with the same brush. We're not all scheming liars. I can't imagine you'd let that put you off ever dating seriously again.'

'You're right. But that wasn't the only thing she was

lying about. She wasn't single or divorced or even separated, she was still very much married, which she'd neglected to mention, and she told me that she spent her weeks off helping her sister care for elderly parents.'

'Another lie?'

Gabe nodded.

'How did she keep her other life a secret?' Sophie asked.

'It was easy, I guess. This was when I was working on the mines and so was she. She worked the same roster as me, two weeks on, two off.'

'And how did you find out the truth?'

'After we'd been dating a while I suggested that we spend our fortnight off together. I'd go with her to meet her parents. She argued against it but I thought I'd surprise her anyway. Turned out I was the one who was surprised. There were no elderly parents but there was a husband—'

'And she never had any intention of leaving him?' Sophie interrupted.

'I don't know. I didn't hang around to find out.'

'You gave up without a fight?' That didn't fit with the Gabe she saw. She liked to imagine him fighting for something he believed in.

'Zara had a husband and a couple of kids. There was no way I was going to be responsible for splitting up a family. My father had an affair when I was quite young. He broke my mother's heart and broke our family apart. Mum never recovered and I didn't want to be the guy who would do that to another family. I didn't want to be my father.'

His story began to make a little more sense now. 'So what did you do?'

'I quit the mine, moved here and tried to put it as far behind me as I could. I told you most of us are running away from something, and that includes me. I'm the last one to give advice on how you need to process what has happened to you and how you should be feeling, so are you sure you don't want me to arrange for you to talk to someone?'

'Talk to someone? Like a psychiatrist, you mean?' Sophie smiled. Maybe Gabe really thought she had lost the plot.

'I was thinking more along the lines of a counsellor.'

'No,' she said, shaking her head. 'Thank you, but I'll be okay. Just remind me to stay away from the red wine while I'm here. Two glasses is obviously making me a bit emotional.'

'Well, if you don't need a counsellor but you just need a friendly hug, I'm here, all right?'

Gabe stood up and Sophie felt like taking him up on his offer right then and there. She could use another one of his hugs but she knew it was dangerous. It was too much too soon and she didn't want to make a mistake. She couldn't afford to fan the spark of attraction just yet. She didn't think she was ready to cope with the consequences.

'Thank you, I'll remember that,' she said, as she saw him to her door.

He'd offered to listen but she didn't think he was ready to hear all her innermost secrets. But she needed to talk to someone. She lifted the lid of her laptop, waking it from its slumber. 'What should I do?' she asked Danny's photo. 'I don't want to forget you, I *won't* forget you, but it felt good to be in Gabe's arms. Is that wrong?'

She picked up the computer and sat it on her lap on her bed. 'Is it too soon to have thoughts like this? Am I reading more into this than I should? What do you think, Danny? Would you like him? I certainly hope I'm not on my own for the rest of my life but should I jump in?'

Danny smiled silently back at her.

'I'm being foolish, aren't I? Gabe hasn't asked me to

jump anywhere. But you would tell me that life goes on. That's something I know you would say. But how soon?'

Sophie shook her head. 'You can't decide for me, can you? It's up to me. I can do whatever I want but I guess if I'm asking for your opinion then maybe I'm not ready. Being here is enough of an adventure. I don't need to complicate things.'

She sighed and shut the laptop. This stint in Antarctica was about her starting again. As a single woman. But when she climbed into bed and closed her eyes it wasn't Danny's goofy smile that she saw. It was a smiling, semi-naked Gabe who kissed her goodnight.

CHAPTER EIGHT

Date: April 1st
Temperature: -15°C
Hours of sunlight: 10.9

To Sophie's dismay, the weather had been declared perfect for the April Fools' Day swim by Gabe, Alex and Michelle, the station's resident meteorologist. Sophie had been hoping it would be delayed as she still wasn't convinced this was a fun, safe, team-bonding activity. It seemed like the sort of silly thing men dreamed up when they were bored, but she had learnt to keep her opinion to herself. Nobody was going to listen to her and unless she declared them all unfit the challenge would take place at some point, if not today then the next perfect day.

She packed up the medical equipment she would need ready to be transported down to the swimming hole at the harbour.

It was a glorious day. Crisp and clear with blue skies and no wind. Goggles were not required but sunglasses were a must. She wore her cold-weather jacket, as had become her habit, but even she didn't need the hood. Either she was acclimatising or the weather was magnificent.

She had checked out the swimming hole a few days earlier to familiarise herself with the situation but she barely recognised it today. Someone had been busy. Inflatable palm trees stood like sentinels at one end and a ladder emerged from the sea water at the opposite end. Folding, plastic beach chairs had been lined up along one edge for the spectators and there was even an inflatable polar bear reclining in one of the chairs. Dom was flipping eggs on the barbecue for bacon and egg muffins and Michelle was making hot chocolate. Anyone who wasn't crazy enough to be taking part in the swim was there to cheer on the hardy souls. There was a celebratory feeling in the air and Sophie found her mood lifting. It was hard to be completely serious when everyone else was getting into the spirit of the occasion.

Alex was the official safety officer and he was stationed by the edge of the hole.

'At least you're sensible,' Sophie said to him.

'Nah, it's just my turn to sit this one out. Someone has to take charge,' he told her in his strong Aussie accent, and Sophie rolled her eyes and decided she was the only sane one in the medical team.

'Just relax, Doc, everything is under control,' he continued, as he picked up a rope and started knotting a loop into one end.

'What's that for?' she asked.

'Before anyone jumps in, I have to tie a rope around them in case I need to pull them out in an emergency. It also means there's no danger of them getting pulled under the ice by any currents or tides.'

The swimming hole looked so much like a pool that Sophie had forgotten it was actually part of the ocean. Her tension kicked up again as she imagined someone being swept out to sea, but before she could voice any concern Alex distracted her.

'Here they come,' he said, and Sophie turned to see a

motley assortment of expeditioners emerging from the temporary hut to parade down to the pool. She'd done a quick, second health check earlier that morning, but the guys had obviously spent the intervening time getting dressed up for the occasion. Finn was wearing board shorts, flippers, a mask and snorkel, Gabe had on a Hawaiian shirt with floral shorts and rubber flip-flops, but Liam took the cake with his mankini outfit. They looked completely ridiculous, so much so that Sophie actually relaxed enough to smile. They looked as though they were headed for the Sydney Mardi Gras, not an icy swim at the bottom of the world.

Finn was first up and he didn't waste any time slipping Alex's rope under his arms and around his chest and jumping in.

'How's the water?' someone called out.

'Friggin' freezing,' came his reply, before he ducked his head under and quickly scrambled out of the pool. One by one they all took their turns and Sophie relaxed more and more as the swims progressed without any disasters.

Finally, only Gabe and Andrew remained.

'You haven't changed your mind, Doc?' Gabe asked, as Andrew stripped down to his shorts.

'About what?'

'The swim. Did you want to join in?'

'Are you kidding?' she said, as Alex tightened the rope around Andrew's chest. 'I'm all for living in the moment but I'm not crazy.'

Andrew jumped into the swimming hole, ducked his head under the water and surfaced beside the ladder. It looked as though he would set the record for the fastest swim of the day but before he could climb out a second head bobbed up out of the water right in front of the ladder.

There was a collective gasp from the crowd as they saw that a Weddell seal had decided to join in the fun.

Andrew turned to grab hold of the ladder and came face to face with the seal. Both the animal and Andrew were equally surprised. The seal dived under the water as Andrew threw himself backwards. He swallowed a mouthful of sea water in the process and sank under the ice.

Alex didn't give him a chance to resurface in his own time. He tugged forcefully on the rope and pulled him back into the swimming hole, clear of the icy shelf. Andrew came out of the water, coughing and spluttering, as Alex hauled him over to the ladder. He managed to get himself out of the pool but he was shivering violently and Sophie wasted no time in hustling him back to the hut to check his obs and get him warmed up again.

Gabe followed them. He wrapped two space blankets around Andrew as Sophie checked his temperature, pulse and blood pressure.

'He's fine,' she told Gabe. 'You'd better go and have your turn before you chicken out.'

By the time Gabe returned from his swim she had sent Andrew back to the red shed to warm up properly.

'How was it?' she asked.

'Cold,' he said, but he was grinning widely and didn't look too uncomfortable. He certainly looked as though he'd fared better than Andrew. He grabbed a towel and Sophie was fascinated by the flexing of his muscles in his chest and arms as he vigorously rubbed himself dry. His wet shorts clung to his legs, showcasing the length and muscle tone. This was the most Sophie had seen of him but she was about to see some more.

He stripped off his shorts to reveal a pair of black trunks that moulded to his sculpted butt. He wrapped his towel around his waist and put his shirt back on, followed by his cold-weather jacket, before swapping his towel for tracksuit pants, until suddenly he was covered up again.

'You look like you enjoyed yourself,' she said, as he sat down beside her to pull on his boots. 'I'm almost sorry I've missed the opportunity. It feels like I might have missed a chance to have a real Antarctic experience.'

'We do another swim in midwinter, on the solstice, you could stay for that.'

Sophie laughed and shook her head. 'I said I was *almost* sorry I missed it. Besides, I won't be here then. You probably haven't had time to check but there was an email from John this morning, confirming that Marianna's surgery was successful and he's planning on returning to Carey on the *Explorer Australis*. He'll be back in three or four weeks.'

Sophie had been disappointed to read John's email. She felt as though she'd barely arrived and she was worried she wasn't going to have time to really experience the ice. She needed to go home a different person.

'So, you're on the downhill stretch?'

'Mmm-hmm.'

'Well, I might have a solution for part of your problem. I'm heading back to the shed for a spa. Why don't you join me? It'll be the closest thing you'll get to the swim.'

'There's really a spa?' She could remember Gabe mentioning it but she couldn't recall seeing one.

'Yep. It's outdoors, just like the swim but the good news is it's heated. It gets fired up on special occasions and this might be your only chance so it would be a shame to miss out on that too. It's quite relaxing.'

Sophie didn't know about relaxing. She was finding it hard to let go when she was wearing almost nothing and sitting mere inches from Gabe, who was also wearing the bare minimum. Even though she'd used all of her fifty-five-kilogram luggage allowance, she hadn't thought to pack bathers so she was wearing a singlet top and a pair of black knickers. She'd tucked her necklace and wedding rings inside the singlet—out of sight, out of mind—but she needn't have bothered. She didn't have room in her head for too many thoughts. Gabe had put his shorts back on but she was very aware of him. It was hard not to be when he took up so much space in the small spa and their knees kept bumping into each other.

Sophie tried to keep to her side of the circular spa but the bubbles and jets had a tendency to push her towards Gabe. Eventually she decided to stop fighting it and let her knees rest against his.

'Are you still regretting missing out on the swim?' he asked her.

'Not really,' she admitted. 'I'm not convinced I would have handled it but there are other things I'd really like to do before I leave. Do you think I'll have a chance to see something away from the station?'

Even though Alex had given his approval for her to operate a quad bike, she still hadn't had time or the opportunity to get out and about.

'The forecast for this week looks good. I have to check a couple of huts before winter really sets in so why don't you come with me?'

The words were out of his mouth before he'd had time to think about what he was asking. He could have easily sent Duncan, the carpenter. In fact, he'd normally send Duncan and one of the mechanics together, but he knew why he was offering—he wanted to spend some time alone with Sophie. Knowing she was now on the countdown to the end of her time in Antarctica made him think about not missing his opportunities. That thought, plus the sensation of her knee against his, made him throw his normal caution to the wind.

He watched her, waiting for her reply. She had piled her hair on top of her head to stop it from getting wet but some tendrils had escaped from the messy bun and the heat of the spa made them curl around her face. She looked young. And beautiful. He'd thought that the first time he'd laid eyes on her too but he'd had other concerns that day. He'd been worried that the AAP were sending him a novice and he knew that he'd judged a book by its cover then. She had been too thin, too beautiful and too young and he had feared the worst. But she'd proved him wrong, showing skills and resilience he hadn't expected and intriguing him along the way. She'd bewitched him with her dimples and her strength of character.

Because of Sophie he'd changed his mind about a lot of things over the past three and a half weeks. Time had become divided in his head to time spent with Sophie and time spent without her. He was normally so cautious but he felt comfortable with her and he could feel her getting under his guard. He knew he should walk away but he couldn't bring himself to do it.

'You look less than impressed, Doc. Doesn't that sound tempting?' he asked, when she didn't immediately jump at his offer.

'I don't want to seem ungrateful but I was hoping for more of an experience, something a bit more...'

'Exciting?'

She looked up at him, lifting her chin and elongating her elegant neck. She was smiling as she replied, 'Interesting.'

She lengthened the word as she ran her eyes over him and he could swear he felt the pressure of her knee increase ever so slightly against his. Was she flirting with him?

'My company's not enough?' he replied, as he fought the urge to pull her towards him and kiss her rosy lips.

'I could have your company at dinner every night without trekking out to look at some huts.'

Yes, she could, and to his ears that sounded pretty enticing, but perhaps she needed more of an incentive. He wanted to spend time with her but that didn't mean that she felt the same way.

'What if I told you that the hut is quite close to a penguin colony and if we're lucky they won't have headed out to sea for the winter yet?'

'That sounds more like it.' She smiled and her dimples winked at him, making him feel like he'd just been awarded a prize. He didn't even worry that he'd made a spur-of-the-moment decision he was so convinced it was the right one.

For the first time in three years he wanted to get to know someone. He wanted to see what would happen.

He couldn't walk away from her. Not any more.

She was skimming her hand across the surface of the water. Backwards and forwards in long sweeping arcs. Her delicate fingers just missed grazing his chest each time she reached past him.

He gave in.

He reached out one hand, blocking her path. His fingers closed around hers and he pulled her towards him. Her knee slid between his and her thigh brushed against him as he tugged her off her seat and onto his lap. Shock waves sparked through his body and a rush of blood flooded his groin. He heard her catch her breath in a little gasp as her breast flattened against his chest.

He waited for her to protest against his actions but she made no other sound.

His erection pressed against the outside of her leg and

her eyes were enormous as she met his gaze. His hand stretched up her back, ready to pull her closer. He needed her closer. He wanted to kiss her. He needed to taste her.

Sophie bent her head and he waited. He wanted her to meet him halfway, he didn't want her to have any regrets. He needed her to want this as much as he did.

But the kiss never came.

Voices drifted across the snow towards them.

'Looks as though we have company,' she said.

She slid off his lap as Finn and Alex came into view. As much as Gabe enjoyed their company, he could quite happily see them both banished to the opposite pole right about now.

Sophie picked up her towel and treated him to a very nice view of her shapely bottom as she climbed out of the spa. But that wasn't enough. Not barely. But that was all he was going to get.

He watched her go. He couldn't follow. He needed to wait for his excitement to subside.

He groaned in frustration but he knew now that it was only a matter of time before the fire that was building between them would consume them both.

CHAPTER NINE

Date: April 5th
Temperature: -11°C
Hours of sunlight: 10.4

SOPHIE GRIPPED THE handles of the quad bike as she concentrated on trying to stay in Gabe's tracks, but she was constantly distracted by the scenery and finding it hard to contain her excitement. Gabe was keeping his promise and the weather had kept her side of the bargain too and Sophie was actually out, with Gabe, exploring the icy continent.

There was only the two of them. She had Gabe to herself for the day. She didn't know what she was more excited about—seeing something of Antarctica or the possibility that she and Gabe might actually cross over the line they'd been dancing on for days. She wasn't going to make the first move, she could never imagine doing that, but if the opportunity presented itself she was going to make sure that she got the kiss she'd been dreaming about. Life was short. She didn't want any more regrets.

The icy plateau stretched for miles on either side of them, flat for the most part, although she could see some distant hills, but the scenery was far from boring. The ice looked smooth but she could feel the swells under her tyres where the wind had formed ripples in the snow that had then frozen into icy waves. The sunlight bounced off the ice, turning the waves a beautiful shade of pale blue, like a shallow tropical sea.

Despite the sunshine and her helmet, gloves and bala-clava, her fingers and cheeks were getting cold by the time they stopped at the first hut. Sophie had pictured wooden huts, like in the days of the old explorers, but, of course, it was just another shipping container. Red, naturally. She thought she would remember the colours of Antarctica as being red, white and blue for ever. Red vehicles, red clothing, red sheds and red S&R pods against a blue and white landscape.

The hut was a smaller version of the buildings at Carey Station. Inside was a small kitchen, a couple of bunk beds and lots of shelving holding loads of crates. Sophie was seeing a different side to life on the ice—a more primi-tive existence but not one without some comforts, but she didn't care. She wouldn't have minded if Gabe had been showing her the garbage collection centre as long as she was getting out and about.

As the station doctor she hadn't expected to have a lot of free time, she had a job to do, but she'd hated to think she might not see anything of her new surroundings be-fore it was time to leave. This was the real Antarctica. The wilderness. The search and rescue had been exciting but she hadn't had time to take in her surroundings. Between the weather conditions obscuring the landscape and the fact that all her concentration and focus had been on her patients and the situation, that day was just a blur in her memory and she wanted to make sure she soaked up every little piece of today.

'There's a check list of things to be done. It's going to take a while,' Gabe said, as he pushed open the door.

The check list was on the wall of the hut, just inside the door. Sophie scanned it. It was a long list.

'Can I help with anything?' She didn't want to miss a minute of the day, and whether it was riding in Gabe's wake, ticking things off a checklist or observing the penguins she was determined to enjoy every minute of the experience.

'Actually, yes. If you want to check the first-aid box, I need a list of any out-of-date items and there should be a list of contents inside the box so see if anything is missing.'

Gabe was moving around the hut, opening and closing vents and examining the structure for any signs of damage. He checked the gas lines, fire extinguishers and tested equipment as Sophie checked the supplies stored in the plastic containers.

Finally they had finished, which meant they could continue on to the penguins. As they crested a ridge Sophie could see a little cove, and filling the icy beach were more penguins than she ever could have imagined. They were huddled together, a huge, seething, dark mass against the ice.

'There must be hundreds of them,' Sophie said, as Gabe switched off his bike and removed his helmet.

'I think it's probably closer to thousands,' he said as he waved her forward. 'Come on.'

Sophie rested her helmet on the seat of her quad bike and said, 'Where are we going?'

'Closer.'

'Won't we frighten them?' They were only a hundred metres or so from the birds now and Sophie wondered how much closer they could get.

Gabe shook his head. 'They're quite fearless and not really fussed about people at any time. The adult penguins need to protect their eggs and newborn chicks from the skua gulls but now that the chicks are so big they don't have any land predators. Leopard seals are their biggest threat and they don't come onto the ice unless they're desperate.'

Having seen how suddenly the Weddell seal had popped up at the swimming hole a few days ago, Sophie wasn't keen on coming face to face with a leopard seal. She moved a little closer to Gabe.

As they got nearer to the colony the mass of black and white gradually separated into more distinguishing features and Sophie was able to make out individual birds. Each penguin had a white shirt front, a black back and black tuxedo tail feathers. At this distance Sophie could see that their beaks were a reddish colour with a black tip—more red!—and they each had a white ring around each eye.

There were thousands of penguins, all identical in their evening finery. They were also taller than she first thought, standing about two feet tall, somewhere in between Emperor penguins and Little penguins, which were the species she was more familiar with. 'What type of penguins are they?'

'Adelie penguins. There are seventeen species of penguins in total but only five call Antarctica home, and you won't see the Adelie anywhere else in the world, only here.'

'Really?'

'Really.'

'Wow.' Sophie thought that was amazing and it made the day even more special.

Gabe stopped by a flat rock only a few metres from the birds, and they sat down to watch. Sophie couldn't believe they could be so close. At this distance the penguins were incredibly loud. They sounded a bit like pigeons crossed with seagulls, cooing and squawking. They were unbelievably loud *and* smelly.

'They look so smart in their feathered tuxedo but they don't smell so great,' she said.

'We're downwind. They've been nesting here since November. That's a lot of penguin poo.'

Sophie laughed. 'That would explain it.'

Amongst the penguins she could see piles of rocks. 'Are those their nests? Those rocks?'

Gabe nodded. 'They build their nests out of rocks, there's quite an art to collecting the best rocks and they like to steal pebbles from each other's nests.'

While that sounded amusing, Sophie thought the finished product looked awfully cold and uncomfortable. A rocky nest sitting on a bed of ice would be cold and difficult to incubate, she imagined. She'd seen Little penguins in Bicheno in Tasmania, and she knew they nested in the grasses on the sand dunes, which seemed far more civilised. She couldn't imagine living on the ice for months at a time.

'The chicks hatch in December,' Gabe explained. 'By February they have their adult feathers and by late March most of the chicks can swim and the penguins will leave the rookery for the pack ice and icebergs and the sea, leaving behind the stone nest. We're lucky to see so many of them still here. By this time next week they could all be gone.'

'You mean you invited me out here, not knowing if they'd still be around?'

Gabe smiled. 'I had to offer you something to get you to keep me company. You weren't too keen on just seeing the hut.'

'You wanted my company?' The idea pleased her, probably more than it should.

'You know the rules, no one goes out alone.'

'Oh.' Sophie was crestfallen. He hadn't needed her specifically. Anyone would have done.

'Relax, I'm joking. I'm glad I got to bring you with me.'

'I'm glad, too,' she admitted. 'I would have hated to miss this.' She pulled her camera out of her pocket and snapped a few photos, before deciding to just enjoy the spectacle and Gabe's company. Who knew when she would have another chance to spend some time alone with him? This was a chance to find out more about him and one of the reasons why she'd been so keen to explore with him today. She looked around her, trying to commit the scene to memory. 'This is just what I imagined Antarctica would be like.'

'The penguins?' Gabe asked.

'All of it—the penguins, the weather, the scenery. It's picture perfect. And untamed. No people around, I feel completely free. It's just what I need.'

It was incredible. She hadn't expected that she could feel so comfortable and relaxed so far from civilisation. It was liberating.

'Would you like to have some time by yourself to take it all in?'

'No. I don't want to be completely alone. If I don't share it with someone then later on it might feel like it wasn't real. I need someone to be able to talk about it with.' That's what she had been missing, someone to share things with. 'I want to share this with you,' she told him. 'Thank you for bringing me here.'

Suddenly, with a lot of squawking, the birds were on the move. Thousands of them. Somehow they all got a simultaneous message that had them heading for the water.

'Can we go closer to the sea?' Sophie asked.

'Sure,' Gabe said as he stood, offered his hand and pulled her to her feet. 'But slowly, okay?'

He led the way and Sophie assumed his caution was to ensure they didn't frighten the birds, but he wasn't paying the penguins any attention. He was looking closely at the ground and she realised he was checking for crevasses and fissures. She hadn't even considered the dangers of crossing the ice. She had been far too caught up in the excitement of the moment. She hadn't expected Gabe to keep her safe, she hadn't even considered that he needed to, but that was exactly what he was doing, and she realised that she wasn't mentally ready for Antarctica and her perils. The excitement of the extraordinary had made her lose focus on the dangers. She was lucky he was with her.

Gabe led her to another rocky outcrop, from where they could watch the penguins dive into the sea. They were moving en masse, the chicks trailing in the wake of their parents. They waddled on their short legs, flapping their wings to maintain their balance on the ice before diving into the ocean. Lots of the chicks hesitated on the shoreline before eventually following the lead of the older birds and plunging into the sea. Sophie could see them skipping through the water, bobbing and diving as they headed out to feed.

By the time the last lot were heading out some were already returning. Most of them shot out of the water and slid along on their bellies several metres before standing up. They walked for a bit and when they grew tired they flopped onto their bellies again and slid forward, pushing themselves along with their feet like little black and white self-propelling skateboards.

They looked hilarious. She pulled her camera out again as she tried to get the perfect photo.

'I could watch them all day,' she said as she turned to

Gabe, only to find out he wasn't beside her. She had a moment of panic before she realised he wouldn't have left her.

She turned further around and found him standing a short distance away on top of a small ridge, facing into the wind. He was standing perfectly still, in profile to her, and she snapped a quick picture of him before a closer look at his expression told her something wasn't right. She looked around her to see if she could pick up any problems. The wind had picked up slightly and the tang of the penguin poo seemed to have lessened. Had she got used to their odour or had the wind direction shifted?

She stood up and went to Gabe. 'What's the matter?'

'I'm not sure. It feels like the temperature has dropped and the wind speed has picked up,' he replied. 'It's probably nothing but I'm just going to put a call in to the station to check the forecast.'

Together they walked back to the quad bikes and Sophie listened while he made the call. A storm was coming. It was headed their way.

'Have they being trying to reach us?'

Gabe shook his head. 'No. We're not due to check in yet and Alex assumed we'd be on our way back by now.'

'Have I held us up?' Sophie had completely lost track of time, she'd been so fascinated by the penguins, and she was concerned that she'd put them in danger.

'No, if it wasn't for the storm we'd have plenty of time, but now it's unlikely we'll make it back to the station. It's too dangerous to try.'

'What will we do?'

'We should have time to make it back to the hut, we can overnight there.'

The intensity of the wind had increased even further and the sun was low on the horizon by the time they reached the hut. Sophie had thought the hut had seemed basic when they'd stopped there earlier, but now that it was their only option she was more than happy to call it home for the night.

Gabe made dinner for them, using a combination of supplies he found in the hut and the contents of the 'rat packs' that they carried in their survival kits. The packs included dried meat, dried vegetables, rice, pasta, soup, chocolate and dried fruit. None of it looked particularly appetising, especially in light of the meals Sophie had grown accustomed to at the station, so she was amazed when Gabe served her a hot three-course dinner. As the wind howled around the hut they feasted by gas lamplight on pumpkin soup with added cumin and dried chives then fried rice with defrosted prawns and veggies, followed by chocolate pudding.

'I wasn't expecting a gourmet meal out here,' she said. 'I can't quite believe that I'm sitting at the bottom of the world, thousands of miles from civilisation as I've always known it, eating a three-course meal. I'm impressed.'

'I aim to please.'

'You never did tell me how you became a chef.'

'Didn't I?'

'No. What got you interested in cooking? It's not a huge secret, is it?' she asked, as she wondered if he was going to stall her again.

'No, it's no secret, it's just not that interesting a story.'

Sophie shrugged. 'We've got all night, and no other entertainment. We may as well tell some stories.'

'Both of us?'

'Yep, but you're going first.' She wasn't going to let him off the hook again. It was time he shared something with her. 'So, come on, spill the beans. Was your mum a good cook?'

* * *

Gabe could think of plenty of other ways to pass the time that didn't involve telling stories but he couldn't suggest most of them. And it looked as though he wasn't going to be able to avoid her questions this time, but he supposed that it would at least get his mind off Sophie. Talking about his mother would remind him of why he was better off alone.

'Cooking wasn't my mum's strong point.' In fact, he couldn't remember his mother cooking anything other than very basic meals—eggs, baked beans on toast, meatloaf. He'd had to learn to feed himself at a young age and he'd started with beans and toast. 'When I was a teenager she had a waitressing job in the local pub. I used to hang out in the kitchen after school and football training and, being a fairly typical teenage boy, I was always hungry. The cook told me that if I wanted to eat I should learn how to cook. It all started there. I didn't love school but I loved cooking. I loved the immediate results and I loved experimenting. I found I had a knack for it and I ended up becoming an apprentice.'

That wasn't the full story but it was enough for now. He didn't think Sophie was ready for the full story, it was something only a few people, including Alex, knew. 'It was just you and your mum?'

'Yep. My father left when I was six and I never saw him again.'

'Never?'

'No.'

'Do you know where he is?'

'No.'

'You haven't tried to find him?'

'He walked out on us. I think I told you before he had an affair?'

Sophie nodded.

'When I was six he chose his girlfriend over his wife and his son. I don't want to find him. There is nothing he and I would have in common. There is nothing I want to have in common with him.' But he knew he always worried that maybe he did share some of his father's traits. Or his mother's. Which would make him either unlovable or a cad. Neither of which were appealing. Both of which confirmed his belief that he was better off alone.

But he didn't want to think or talk about his mother or his father. He preferred to think about Sophie.

'Not everyone has a happy childhood. I certainly didn't and I try not to think about it too much. It's all behind me now.' He said as he steered the conversation back to her family. As he'd hoped, Sophie let the topic lie then and he successfully managed to avoid any further discussion about his past for the rest of the evening.

Gabe woke suddenly. He was disoriented and unsure why he'd woken. It took a moment to get his bearings. The shape of the furniture was wrong and the ceiling was too close to his head. The room was bathed in a pale green light. He turned his head to his left, looking for the time and expecting to see the display of his docking station. There was a green glow but it was different from the LED light from his docking station, and then he remembered. He was in the hut. With Sophie. He was on the top bunk and the green light wasn't coming from an electrical source but through the window.

He knew what it was but he also knew it wasn't the glow that had woken him. It was the absence of noise. The wind had dropped completely. There wasn't a sound except for Sophie's breathing. The weather had cleared, leaving behind the silence that only a world blanketed in snow had.

He got up and pulled his clothes on before waking Sophie.

'Doc?'

Sophie stirred. 'What is it? What's wrong?'

'Nothing. There's something I want you to see.'

'It's the middle of the night,' she said, rubbing her eyes.

'I know. Get dressed. You'll want to see this.'

'What's that light?'

'If you get dressed I'll show you.'

He tried not to watch as she swung her legs out of the bed. She'd been sleeping in her thermal leggings and a T-shirt. It was definitely not sexy lingerie but somehow she managed to make it look hot. She had undone her plaits and her hair fell over her shoulders in dark waves. He could see the swell of her breasts under the thin wool of her top. The hut was warm but the air in the room was obviously colder than the air in her sleeping bag and he saw her nipples peak as her body registered the change in temperature.

He moved away and occupied himself by putting the kettle on while she got dressed, but he was still only inches away from her and her scent filled the hut. Warm and sweet. It was intoxicating. Sophie had really turned his world upside down. He hadn't expected her and having her so close and without anyone else around was proving torturous. He needed to keep some perspective. He needed to remember that he'd lost everyone he'd ever cared about and he was better off alone.

But that didn't stop him from thinking about her. It didn't stop him from imagining the lines of her body, the softness of her skin, the touch of her fingers.

He heard her feet hit the floor as she stood up from the bottom bunk and he imagined he could feel the air moving as she pulled on her clothes.

He opened the door as she finished putting her boots on and together they stepped outside. The sky glowed green and Gabe heard Sophie's intake of breath as she looked up and stretched out a hand as if to touch the lights that danced above their heads. From one edge of the night sky to the other long fingers of light shimmered and glowed. The dark night sky had been overtaken by rich emerald green swirls tinged with sapphire blue and gold.

The lights were bright enough to obscure the stars, which were dulled by the magnificence of the aurora australis.

Sophie turned in a circle to follow the lights as they danced across the sky. 'It looks like the world has been turned upside down. I've seen these colours in the ocean but never in the sky.' The colours were crisp and clear, translucent, and she lifted her hand again as if to reach out to touch them. 'They are so beautiful.' They shone like phosphorescence, splitting the darkness like laser beams. A curtain of coloured smoke wafting across the sky. 'You've seen the lights before?'

'Yes, but every time they're different. So every time is like the first time.' He knew he wouldn't forget seeing the lights tonight but it was the company that made them special.

'It's amazing.'

'Do you want to get your camera?'

She shook her head. 'No. I don't think I could do it justice. I just want to sit and enjoy it.'

Gabe brought cushions from the hut and put them side by side on the steps. The steps were narrow and Sophie was pressed up against him as they watched the display.

He could feel the length of her thigh against his and he imagined he could feel her body heat even through the thick insulated suits. Indecent thoughts had been running through his head ever since he had enticed her out of bed and now that she was practically sitting in his lap his thoughts were getting more and more R-rated. Despite the fact they were both bundled up in myriad layers of clothing, he could picture her shape and he could see her face under the emerald glow of the Southern Lights and that was enough to keep his blood boiling.

'What causes the lights?' she asked him, and her question focussed his attention but also gave him a reason to look at her. She had left her hair loose and the dark curls were poking out from beneath her beanie, spilling over the front of her red suit like a chocolate fountain.

He resisted the urge to reach out and lift the weight of her hair in his hands as he replied, 'How technical do you want me to be, Doc?'

He added her title deliberately to remind himself of who she was. She was a colleague, a fellow expeditioner, she wasn't a random woman who he'd met in a bar and could spend the weekend with. He couldn't afford to indulge his fantasies. He needed to remind himself of who she was and where they were. Having Sophie around was making him rethink his self-imposed rule of not fooling around with colleagues but no matter how much he might want to test the boundaries he couldn't pretend that it would be a good idea, for either of them, but particularly for her. He couldn't imagine that she was emotionally ready for any sort of relationship other than a platonic one.

'I'm a science geek. Give me your best.' She smiled and her dimples flashed and almost destroyed his resolve.

He was sorely tempted to give her his best but he thought it might not end as he wished. Instead, he looked up at the sky, making sure to keep temptation out of sight, as he answered her. 'There are millions of particles in the galaxy; debris, magnetic waves, radiation; which together are generally called a solar wind. They stream off the sun and are drawn to the Earth's magnetic poles.'

'So that's why you see them at the poles? Because of the magnetic fields?'

'Yes, but we only see the lights here in winter because there's too much sunlight during the rest of the year.'

'What makes the different colours?'

'The particles energise the gases in our atmosphere and cause them to release colours of light. The different gases release different colours. When the particles collide with oxygen you'll see yellow and green, while nitrogen will produce red, violet and blue.'

'I think you might be a secret science geek too,' Sophie laughed.

'Why do you say that?'

'You used to cook for a living—cooking can be quite a scientific process—and you had all those penguin facts on the tip of your tongue today, and now this lesson on the universe. You're definitely a science geek.'

'You have to admit penguins are fascinating. I made it my business to learn about them but I suppose there's some merit to your argument. If I'd been more interested in schoolwork then science might have been my thing, but I ended up in a kitchen.'

'And now you're here.' Sophie waved one arm expansively towards the dark horizon and the green sky above them. 'I can see how being here could become addictive. There's nowhere else quite like it, is there?'

'No, it's hard to give up,' he agreed. He missed the ice whenever he left for a break. He was attracted to the wildness and the freedom of Antarctica. It really was the last frontier. Of course, there were rules, particularly in terms of safety, but the expeditioners were a little community at the bottom of the earth, remote and separate from the rest of the world, and that was one of the things he relished.

Sophie was still gazing heavenward as the display continued in all its spectacular glory. 'It's almost impossible to believe that the lights are naturally occurring. Looking up at this sky, I can understand why people believe in extra-terrestrials and alien life forms.'

'There are lots of superstitions associated with the lights. The Northern Lights were thought to be an omen of war or destruction.'

'But they're so beautiful,' she sighed. 'I had the impression that Antarctica was red, white and blue, but now I'll remember it as emerald and gold.'

He felt her leg twitch as she shivered. 'Are you cold?'

'A little.'

'Do you want to go inside?'

'I don't think I can leave yet.'

He knew how she felt. The first experience with the lights was truly magical and he didn't want to break the spell by putting an end to the night. 'Stand up and move around then, get your blood pumping, and I'll bring you something warm to drink.'

Sophie followed Gabe into the hut. She had decided to fetch her camera. If she was going to have a few moments alone she thought she'd try to capture the display. She snapped a few photos but it wasn't long before her batteries succumbed to the cold and the camera was useless. She slipped it into her pocket as Gabe returned with hot drinks and blankets.

He handed her a mug of steaming hot chocolate before wrapping the blanket around her shoulders. She held it in place with one hand as Gabe sat beside her and wrapped the other end around his back. The blanket brought them closer together and now not only was her thigh pressed against his but she was leaning her shoulder against his too.

She sipped the hot chocolate and tried to ignore the feeling of intimacy that sitting so close to Gabe evoked. She could feel the firmness of his body and she could smell a hint of cinnamon underlying the chocolate smell. Was that Gabe? She'd never noticed that before.

'This tastes amazing.' The hot chocolate was unlike anything she'd ever tasted. Was it the location, the experience or the circumstances that was making it taste so heavenly?

'It's my secret ingredient,' he told her.

'What did you put in it?'

'If I told you it wouldn't be a secret any more, would it?'

'I promise not to tell a soul.'

He grinned. 'In that case, it's chilli and cinnamon powders.'

'Really? You're caving in that easily? You're not even going to make me beg?'

'What can I say? I'm a sucker for a pretty face.'

Sophie was slightly disappointed to hear that the cinnamon smell was coming from the drink and not from Gabe but his comment perked her up.

'Did you get any good photos?' he asked.

'I doubt it. It's impossible to do the sky justice but I had to try to capture it. It's a bit like the penguins today. I'm worried that once I leave and no one else I know has seen this it will seem less real. I wanted to try to capture it because if I'm not going to have anyone to share it with I want some way of remembering. I came to the ice to figure out how to be on my own again and this is one of those times when it hits home that I really am alone. But I'll be okay. Given time.'

She wasn't here to forget but to move on. She wanted to make a new start. She wanted new memories and sitting under the Southern Lights, drinking hot chocolate, was exactly the type of new memory she wanted. She would never see this anywhere else and now, whenever she thought of the Southern Lights, she would associate them with Gabe. Tonight would be a perfect memory.

Gabe stood up as they finished their drinks and reached for her hand. 'Time to get warm,' he said, as he pulled her to her feet.

They were standing almost chest to chest and Sophie tipped her head back to look up at him. 'Thank you,' she said. 'It's been a perfect day.'

Gabe's eyes were dark. He wasn't smiling but he was watching her so intensely that she could feel a yearning in her belly as though a fire was being stoked. She leant towards him as if she was the aurora and he was the South Pole. She was powerless to resist the pull of attraction. She put her hands on his chest and even through his thick jacket she could feel his strength. He felt solid and dependable and masculine.

She felt his arms wrap around her as he pulled her in even closer. He bent his head.

'Sophie.'

Her name was a whisper on his lips.

It was the first time in weeks she had been called anything other than 'Doc' and she liked the way her name sounded when he said it. It made her heart sing.

And then the whisper was gone as his lips covered hers.

His beard was rough against her cheek but the contrast between the coarseness of his beard and the softness of his lips was incredible. Her breath escaped in a sigh as she closed her eyes and opened her mouth to him.

He tasted of cinnamon and chocolate and she knew she would always associate those flavours with Gabe.

It was amazing to kiss someone when the only thing you could feel was their mouth. Her hands were on his chest but because of all their layers the only exposed parts of them were their noses and lips. It concentrated her senses and sharpened her focus. Everything she could touch and feel was going into the kiss. Everything she could touch and feel was happening through her lips.

She melted into him, unable to tell where she stopped and he started. This was the kiss she'd been dreaming of but it was better than she'd imagined. Gabe's lips were soft but his tongue was searching and as he explored her mouth a rush of heat shot from her chest to her belly and all the way to her toes. It was intense, powerful and all-consuming. It was an incredible feeling, but did that make it right?

Sophie wasn't sure. She pulled away, pushing her hands against his chest until their lips came apart.

'What's wrong?'

'I didn't mean to kiss you.'

'I think you'll find I kissed you,' he replied without a trace of apology in his voice. 'And I meant to. I'm sorry if I made you feel uncomfortable but you looked so beautiful that I couldn't help it. It seemed like a perfect way to end a perfect day.'

'Don't apologise.' Sophie shook her head, even though she agreed with him. It had felt perfect. 'You didn't make me feel uncomfortable. I enjoyed it, that's not the problem. If I'm honest I've been thinking about what it would be like to kiss you for days.'

'So we're on the same page.' He grinned. 'That's good news.'

'Except that technically you could be considered my patient.'

'I don't think the same rules apply in Antarctica.'

'All the staff are potentially my patients and I shouldn't overstep the boundaries. It's part of the oath I took.'

'I promise not to get sick while you're here. If you're not treating me for anything then surely that's okay?'

It was a flimsy argument but Sophie was tempted to go with it.

'I'm not sure.' The kiss had been so lovely it was going to be hard to stop. It had made her feel alive again. It had made her happy. She wasn't sure how ready she was for this but it felt perfect. They were in a world of their own. A world away from everything else. It was just the two of them and it was very tempting to ignore protocol. After all, who would ever know?

Gabe bent his head. 'I promise I won't tell anyone.' She could feel his words caress her cheek, making her knees go weak. 'But I don't want you to have any regrets. This has to be your decision.'

She didn't want to resist.

'And there's only one decision you need to make,' Gabe continued. 'Either you want to explore this thing between us or you don't. But you don't need to make that decision tonight. I'm not going anywhere but you do need to go to bed. I can stop now but if you don't go inside and go to bed I might not be able to stop again.'

Sophie lay her in bunk underneath Gabe's, trying to breathe quietly. Trying to sleep. But it was going to be impossible. Her mind kept replaying that kiss.

She'd expected to feel guilty but there was no denying she had wanted to kiss him. That she'd wanted to for days.

It wasn't wrong and she wasn't going to feel guilty about something that felt so right. She was done feeling guilty.

Sitting under that magical sky had made her feel small and insignificant. It had put things into perspective for her and reminded her that they were all temporary. The lights would be there long after she and everyone else she knew had gone. The lights would bathe the world in their colours for eternity but she only had the here and now. She only had one chance at life and she needed to live it.

Life was short. She needed to be brave.

She wanted to be fearless. She needed to take a chance and live each moment. She didn't know how many she had left and she didn't want to waste any of them.

He'd said it was her decision.

She wanted to feel alive. She wanted to feel happy.

She wanted to share this night with Gabe.

She wanted to live her life without regrets.

It was her decision and she was willing to take a chance.

Sophie tugged her necklace over her head. She stuffed the chain and her wedding rings into the pocket of her fleece and whispered to Gabe, 'Are you awake?'

CHAPTER TEN

Date: April 6th
Temperature: -12°C
Hours of sunlight: 10.3

SOPHIE HUGGED HER memories of last night to her like a secret. Coming to Antarctica had been the right decision. She felt like the old Sophie. Happy. Light. Floating. Free.

She coasted through the morning. The return trip to the station passed by in a blur. Not even the scenery could distract her from her thoughts, which were filled with memories of last night, snapshots of a day in her life. A day she wasn't going to forget in a hurry, if ever. The spectacle of the lights, the colours of the universe and the stillness of the early morning when all she'd been able to hear had been the sound of Gabe's breathing.

The heat of Gabe's kisses and the touch of his embrace had set her free from the past. She wasn't going to forget Danny but she knew now that she would be able to move on.

Gabe was only the second man she'd ever slept with, and while she'd expected it to be different she hadn't really thought about it being better. But in many ways it had been. She'd got more than she'd bargained for but she wasn't complaining. Perhaps the anticipation had made it all the more sweet or perhaps Gabe's experience had been the difference. She'd been smouldering for days, on edge as she'd tried to ignore their attraction, all while hoping she'd eventually have a chance to explore it, and Gabe's kisses had been the spark that had stoked her fire and set her alight. Her skin tingled with the memory of his touch and her muscles ached from the exercise.

Back at the station she turned on her laptop, ready to download her photos. Danny's photo popped up on the screensaver, his goofy smile filling the screen.

'I'm sorry, Danny, it just felt right. Can you understand?'

She didn't really feel as though she needed to apologise for being happy, and she didn't want to dwell on Danny so she clicked an icon to open a program and the screensaver and Danny's photo disappeared from view.

She loaded her photos and scrolled through them, searching for one that she could use as a new screensaver. There were a couple of good ones of the penguins, a gorgeous one of Gabe in profile that she'd snapped just before the storm warning and one sensational shot of the Southern Lights. She chose that one. It reminded her of Gabe, without actually being him. She wasn't ready to replace Danny's photo with one of Gabe, it was far too early for such an extreme measure, but she didn't want to see Danny smiling at her if she was thinking about someone else. Danny would always be in her heart but he was only a memory now. Gabe was living, breathing, warm and real. His arms could hold her and touch her and she missed the touch of another person.

Her email was flashing, indicating new messages. She clicked on her inbox and found a message from Luke. She waited for a stab of guilt as she read his email but she felt nothing but happiness. She was done feeling guilty. Guilt wasn't going to bring Danny back.

She sent Luke a quick, innocuous reply and attached her two best penguin photos. She thought about attaching one of the Southern Lights but decided she didn't want to share that moment with anyone other than Gabe. That was their thing. She knew there wouldn't be too many things she would share with him, there wasn't time. She was due to leave in three weeks and she wanted to keep something of Gabe just for herself.

CHAPTER ELEVEN

Date: April 19th
Temperature: -6°C
Hours of sunlight: 8.7

SOPHIE WAS HAPPY. Antarctica had given her back her old self. It had given her Gabe and she had spent the past fortnight making memories with him that would sustain her through any dark moments.

She had to make memories, that was all she would be taking with her when she left. Gabe hadn't made her any promises. She knew how he felt about serious relationships. He didn't do commitment and that was fine with her. She wasn't ready for anything more either. She would have been happy with one incredible night but they'd had two weeks. She hadn't expected to find such happiness down here but she was going to grab it with both hands. She had blossomed under Gabe's touch. She was happy again She laughed, she ate, she sang in the shower and walked around with a silly smile on her face. She knew that by the time she left she would be well on her way to healing. She knew she'd be able to move on. Gabe had shown her that, he was the proof she needed.

But he was her secret. She wasn't ready to share what they had with anyone else on the station. She didn't need to share him and it was easy to keep their status private. They were the only two who had their dongas on the ground floor of the red shed and being side by side meant it wasn't difficult to move between their rooms. The only difficulty was squeezing two of them into the narrow bed but, as Gabe had said, where there's a will there's a way, and Sophie enjoyed having to snuggle against him to avoid tumbling out of bed. They fitted together well and she loved being in his arms.

Over the past two weeks she had stopped thinking about everything in contrast to Danny. Life at Carey had become about her and Gabe. Danny wasn't constantly in her thoughts any more. She was surviving without him. She could look to the future again and it no longer seemed quite so bleak.

When she hadn't been sneaking into Gabe's room she had been kept busy with routine medical procedures and examinations. A foreign body in an eye, a back strain, an episode of chest pain, which had thankfully turned out to be indigestion, and stitches in Liam's chin. As she had stitched him up yesterday she'd realised that by the time the stitches would need removing she would be gone. Dr John would be the one to take them out. Her time was flying past. The supply ship, the *Explorer Australis*, was well on its way, making its last voyage down south before winter really closed in. The ship had left Douglas Station and was on her way to Carey. Sophie was into her last week.

She snuggled closer to Gabe, tucking her leg over his, seeking his warmth, as she began to make the most of one of her last mornings.

Gabe was lying in bed, watching her get dressed. She was standing in her underwear and had just pulled a T-shirt over her head when Gabe's door flew open and Finn burst in to the room.

'Gabe, there's been an accident—' Sophie saw Finn's double-take when he saw her standing semi-naked in the middle of the floor but he recovered quickly. 'Doc, good you're here. I need you too.' He might have made a quick recovery but she didn't miss the quizzical look he gave Gabe.

Gabe didn't bother explaining. There were more important things to worry about. He threw back the covers and grabbed a pair of boxer shorts as he asked, 'How bad?'

'One casualty. It's Alex.'

Sophie noticed Gabe's slight hesitation and his hand was shaking as he pulled his shorts up. Sophie knew how close he and Alex were. They were like brothers. Gabe looked at Finn.

'He's alive but unconscious,' Finn said. 'A forklift reversed into some shelving in the storage shed, knocking it down onto Alex.' Finn looked at Sophie. 'We're lifting it off but we don't want to move him.'

Sophie sprang into action. This was her department now. 'I need a spinal board and my emergency kit. Come with me,' she directed Finn.

She collected everything she thought she might need, threw on her cold-weather jacket and pants and followed Finn to the storage shed. Gabe had beaten them there and was overseeing the logistics of removing a heavy metal storage unit that had crushed Alex.

Alex was lying on his back. The shelving unit had fallen across his chest and left shoulder, pinning him to the floor. Sophie knelt beside him and put her hand gently on his right shoulder.

'Alex?' There was no response. He was still unconscious and she could see a pool of blood under his head. But he was breathing.

Gabe and the other men had cleared away the debris that had fallen from the shelves and were looking at her, waiting for her okay to move the toppled unit. She nodded. She knew it had to be done, she just hoped it wasn't going to present her with more problems.

Time was of the essence and she worked quickly once the area was clear. Alex's pupils reacted equally to torchlight, his blood pressure was low and his heart rate was elevated, but nothing too worrying. Carefully she fixed a cervical collar around his neck before getting Gabe and Finn to help her assemble the spinal board around him. Then they made their way slowly and cautiously back to the red shed.

Gabe refused to leave Alex's side, choosing instead to remain in the clinic while Sophie took X-rays and tried her best to assess the extent of his injuries.

'Is he going to be all right?'

'I can't tell you. I have to develop the X-rays and it depends how long he takes to regain consciousness. His pupils are reacting equally so I don't think there's any intracranial bleeding. We can be thankful that the blood is flowing out, not in. I'm sorry but we'll just have to wait and see.' She knew that wasn't what Gabe wanted to hear but it was all she could tell him at the moment.

'Alex is like family to me.'

'I know, and I'll do everything I can.'

'I've lost everyone I've ever cared about.'

Sophie was shaving some of Alex's blond curls so she could stitch his head wound, but she paused briefly to squeeze Gabe's hand. She wanted to stop what she was doing to comfort Gabe but she couldn't. She had to take care of Alex first.

'Everyone?' she asked.

'My father and my mother.'

Sophie knew his father had walked out when Gabe had been young but she hadn't realised he'd lost his mother too. They had been spending every spare minute together but she realised that while she knew him intimately in a physical sense there was a lot he hadn't shared with her. She had tried to get him to open up but he was very adept at changing the subject. She wondered what had happened. He knew her whole life story and she still knew almost nothing about him.

'Do you want to talk about it? You listened to me unload about Danny, it's my turn to listen now.'

'It's a long story.'

'I'm not going anywhere.'

'I'm not really sure exactly where it starts.'

Gabe paused and Sophie thought that he wasn't going to say anything more. She kept stitching, giving him some time, and he eventually continued.

'There are lots of interwoven events and one of them must have come first but I think I was too young to know which one that was. I remember my father coming and going, but only vaguely, when I was a pre-schooler. I don't know if he was around a lot when I was younger but he walked out for good when I was six. I found out years later he'd had an affair. More than one. Mum suffered from depression but I don't know whether that started before or after the affairs. She might have been difficult to live with but that didn't give him the right to be unfaithful. Mum made him choose between us and his latest girlfriend and he didn't pick us. That was the end of our family.'

Sophie's heart ached for the six-year-old Gabe. 'And your mum? What happened to her?' She knew he felt as though his father had abandoned him and she had to agree but surely his mother had been there for him? If not, it would explain a lot more about him. She continued to stitch Alex's head wound, taking her time now, not because it was difficult but because she was worried that if she stopped she might break Gabe's concentration. It was almost as though he was talking to himself, as though he'd forgotten she was there, and she didn't want to interrupt his train of thought.

'Mum struggled to cope after that and when I was seven I was put into foster-care for the first time. When Mum felt like she had things under control again I was sent back to live with her and that pattern kept repeating right through to my teenage years. I was in and out of foster-care and I hated it. I became an angry, rebellious teenager. As far as I could see, there wasn't any point to anything. School, friendships, everything could change in an instant. Sometimes it would be Mum's decision, she'd just pack us up and leave, convinced that starting somewhere new would be the answer, and other times I'd change schools depending on which foster-family I was sent to. I had a very unsettled existence, physically and emotionally, and I think I was heading for big trouble.

'If it wasn't for one particular teacher I had when I was fourteen, I know I wouldn't have made it. That teacher got me into football and it was around that time that Mum got the job waitressing in the pub. It wasn't an exceptional job but her boss was fantastic. I got to hang out in the kitchen after school and football training. I loved being in the kitchen and I loved cooking, but it was the attention and time that Mum's boss gave me that made the difference. He owned the pub but food was his passion and he was the chef. He taught me how to cook. Cooking and football gave me a purpose.'

Sophie had heard part of this story before but Gabe had

certainly kept a lot of the detail from her the first time. He'd made it sound so simple and straightforward and commonplace that night in the hut.

'I was happy but too wrapped up in my own teenage world to notice that Mum was unhappy. When I was sixteen she took her own life. I lost it then for a while. I was sixteen and on my own. All my family were gone.'

Sophie bit back tears as her heart broke for Gabe. 'What did you do?'

'I dropped out of school. But Mum's boss stepped in. He offered me an apprenticeship in the pub, along with lodgings, and because I was sixteen I was allowed to live independently. That was my chance and I took it. I've been on my own ever since.'

'What about Zara?' Sophie knew he'd been invested in that relationship. It hadn't worked out but he *had* made an effort to have a relationship, he hadn't always been alone.

'Zara just confirmed it for me. Relationships aren't worth it. Someone always loses. It was my mother and then me.'

'Maybe you just haven't found the right person yet.'

Gabe shook his head. 'I'm better off on my own.'

Sophie was bandaging Alex's wound. 'No one is better off alone.'

Gabe's words were upsetting her. It wasn't the first time he'd mentioned being better off alone. His childhood experiences went a long way to explain why he felt the way he did, but surely he couldn't think it meant he should spend the rest of his life on his own? He couldn't really mean it, could he? Her relationship with Danny hadn't worked out as she'd expected, but she'd rather have loved Danny than not, and she was positive she would find love again. What was the point in living your life alone?

She was upset but she tried not to show it. Even though

she should have known better, she realised she'd been thinking about the future, a future with Gabe. She had fallen hard and fast but she could see she was being unrealistic, given the fact that she would be leaving soon and Gabe had said nothing about a future together. It was obvious now how different his intentions were from hers but she still needed to look forward. She didn't plan on being on her own for ever, even if Gabe did.

But he had shown her that she could be happy again. That she could love and laugh. He didn't see the same future but there was still one out there for her. She no longer thought in terms of years—her days of making three-year plans were over—but she was feeling better about what was ahead, even if Gabe wouldn't be there to share it with her. She would take little steps, a day, a week, a month at a time, and she would start again when she got home.

She felt confident about returning to the real world. Hopefully, the real world was ready for her.

Date: April 20th
Temperature: -5°C
Hours of sunlight: 8.6

'Well, well, if it isn't the dark horse himself.'

Alex was lying flat on his back in the hospital bed but his greeting to Gabe was robust.

'You're feeling better, I take it,' Gabe said, as he pulled a chair to the side of the bed and sat down.

'Battered and bruised with a bit of a headache, but I'm an old rugby player with a noggin like a brick. It takes more than a collapsed shelf to knock me off. But I reckon there's more interesting things to discuss than the state of my head.'

'Like?'

'Like what's the deal with you and Sophie? How long has that been going on?'

'A couple of weeks.'

Alex raised an eyebrow. 'When were you going to tell me?'

'Dunno. It's no big deal.' Alex was like a brother to Gabe, they'd formed a close friendship on the ice, and no topic, including women, was normally off-limits between them. But Gabe felt differently about Sophie. Their relationship was private and he would have preferred it if it had stayed that way. It was his way of protecting his emotional investment. In his opinion, the fewer people who knew about the relationship the better. It would hurt less if he wasn't expected to talk about his feelings when it ended. 'It just happened.'

'Nice try, Romeo. I think you're forgetting who you're talking to. I know you. Nothing just happens with you. So what's next?'

'Nothing. She's leaving with the ship in a few days.'

'You're letting her go?'

Gabe shrugged.

'You're kidding!'

'What other option do I have?'

'Ask her to stay.'

'I can't.'

'Can't or won't?'

'Won't.'

'Reason?'

'She's said she needs to learn to be on her own.'

'And you're happy to leave it at that? There's enough heat between the two of you to power this place if our generators went down, it was only a matter of time before one of you had to make a move. I can't believe you're happy to let her walk away.'

'It's not up to me. It's her decision.'

Gabe didn't want to say goodbye. Their relationship had begun simply enough. Sophie was aware of his penchant for short-term involvement, his aversion to commitment, and she'd said it was all she wanted at this stage in her life too. There wasn't any other option. Her time on the ice was finite. It was short and sweet or nothing. The problem was that his vision of his future had changed since meeting her. He could picture a future with her and it seemed far less bleak and solitary than any other future he could imagine. But he wasn't sure if now was the right time to tell her that, and he couldn't risk putting his heart on the line. Not yet. He didn't think Sophie was ready to hear how he was feeling. She'd said she needed to learn to be on her own and he didn't think she was there yet. He was just temporary in her life.

But it was rather ironic that this was the one time when he wished that temporary wasn't an option.

CHAPTER TWELVE

Date: April 23rd
Temperature: -11°C
Hours of sunlight: 8.3

SOPHIE HAD BEEN packed and ready to leave for the past two days, but neither she nor Gabe had spoken about what happened next. It was almost as if, by ignoring the inevitable, they could pretend it wasn't real. And that was how their relationship felt to Gabe. Like a fairy-tale.

But it looked as if the fairy-tale would last a little longer. The *Explorer Australis* had been due to dock at Carey yesterday but it was stuck in pack ice off the coast. Gabe didn't mind. It meant he would have the pleasure of Sophie's company for another day but any longer than a few more days without the ship and they would need to put other plans in place. The ship would need to start its return journey before winter really closed in, but the station was waiting on vital supplies and a dozen expeditioners, including Sophie, were waiting to leave. If the ship couldn't get any closer, arrangements would have to be made to chopper supplies in and people out. The ship had picked up helicopters from Douglas Station, they would spend winter on the mainland, but at least that gave them an alternative transport option. Gabe needed to discuss the weather forecast with Michelle. If the ship wasn't going to be able to break through the ice they needed to find a window of favourable weather in which to fly the choppers.

But their resident meteorologist couldn't give Gabe the forecast he wanted. 'There's a big storm front coming,' Michelle told him. 'More cold weather and strong winds. There's no chance of flying the choppers for the next twenty-four hours. The winds are likely to increase and could be in excess of one hundred and fifty kilometres an hour. I think we need to batten down the hatches here and prepare to wait this one out. No one is going anywhere.'

'How long have we got before it hits?'

'Another hour before it starts, another hour after that before it really cranks up.'

'All right, I need to call everyone back to the red shed.' Fortunately, everyone was at the station, they'd been doing the final pack up in preparation for winter so everyone was close to hand, but Gabe wanted them all together. He needed to know they were all safe and accounted for.

He spent the next hour organising for the station to be storm-proofed. Anything that wasn't required was packed away or tied down until one by one everyone had finished and had assembled in the mess hall, but when he did a head count Sophie was missing.

'Does anyone know where she is?'

'If she's not in her clinic then most likely in the hydroponics shed,' came Dom's reply.

'I'm going to get her,' Gabe said. 'No one is to leave the shed.'

Sophie was his responsibility. He needed to see her. He needed to keep her safe.

She was picking lettuces when he found her.

'Soph.' He no longer called her 'Doc'. He had stopped

thinking about her as the doctor, she had taken on a whole new meaning for him. 'There's a big storm coming, we need to get back to the red shed.'

She didn't argue and he waited while she packed away her gardening tools, but when he opened the door he found that the weather had turned in the few minutes he'd been inside the shed. The wind had picked up and was howling between the buildings. The snow was swirling, making whiteout conditions, and the red shed was no longer visible. He shut the door and turned to Sophie. She had pulled on her cold-weather jacket and gloves but had no eye protection.

'Do you have your goggles with you?' he asked.

'No.' She shook her head. 'Just sunglasses.'

Sunglasses weren't going to cut it. Not in these conditions. He opened the first-aid cabinet that was fixed to the wall beside the door and rummaged around for a spare pair. He handed them to her.

'Put these on. The weather's deteriorated. Pull your neck warmer up too,' he said, as he pulled the hood of her jacket over her head and tightened it around her face until all that could be seen of her was her nose. He kissed the tip of her nose before opening the door and reaching for the guide rope. He took her hand and wrapped it around the rope. 'That leads to the red shed. Don't let go of it.' He could see a look of uncertainty and nervousness in her green eyes as her fingers tightened around the rope. 'It's okay,' he reassured her, 'I'll be right behind you.'

The wind was ferocious and even Gabe struggled to keep his feet as they stepped out from the shelter of the building. He made sure he stayed only inches from Sophie, worried he would lose sight of her. They had their heads bent as they leant into the wind. He was almost doubled over and he wondered if they should have clipped themselves to the guide rope. Station policy stated that they just needed to hold on but he couldn't recall ever encountering such strong winds before.

He could taste the saltiness of the ocean in the ice that stung his cheeks and melted on his tongue. The wind was blowing straight off the harbour, lifting the water off the tops of the waves and freezing it as it blew it over the land.

Sophie slipped on the ice and Gabe grabbed her around the waist with one arm, struggling to keep his balance and at the same time trying to help her stay on her feet without completely letting go of the rope. She regained her footing and they battled on. They were only halfway there but Gabe could feel his legs becoming fatigued, it was exhausting. And that was when the mistake was made.

He saw Sophie lift her head, which exposed her chest to the wind. It was the wrong thing to do but before he could tell her to tuck her head down the wind blasted into her and knocked her feet out from under her. Although the scene seemed to play out in slow motion Gabe's reaction time wasn't fast enough and he watched helplessly as the wind ripped the rope from her hands.

'Sophie!'

Her name was torn from his lips and flung away on the wind. He let go of the rope, reaching out for her instinctively, and suddenly there was nothing.

The wind took him too and flung him across the ice. He was tumbling. He was falling. He had no way of knowing which way was up and which way was down. He had no sense of direction. He had nothing.

No Sophie. No station. Nothing.

In a split second they had been torn apart.

In the blink of an eye they had both vanished.

Sophie cried out as she felt the rope tear from her grasp but she never heard the words as the wind ripped them straight from her lips and flung them away. Her words were no match for the force of the wind. Neither was she.

The wind took her as well. She spun through the air before crashing onto the ice. She could hear her suit scraping on the ice as she was blown backwards. She tumbled over and over as she flung her arms out, desperately seeking for something to grab hold of even though she knew there was nothing there.

She lost all sense of time and space. The world was white. To her dizzy brain there was no way of discerning between the ice and the sky. It was all the same.

There was nothing she could do. There was no way of stopping. She knew there was nothing out here. Nothing but a vast, icy plateau. She'd seen it.

So this was it.

This was how it was all going to end.

She would become just another soul lost at the bottom of the world.

'Where are they?' Alex peered over Finn's shoulder, searching for a glimpse of Gabe and Sophie. They were taking longer than he'd expected to make their way back to the red shed and he was starting to worry.

'I see them,' Finn said, as the red of Sophie's jacket came into view through the sleet.

Alex could see her now. He could see her struggling to keep her balance. He held his breath as she stumbled and he saw Gabe grab her around the waist to steady her.

He saw her lift her head and watched in slow motion as her feet were blown out from underneath her, but this time Gabe didn't have a chance to grab her. Alex watched, horrified, as the wind whipped her away. He saw Gabe reach for her but he was too late and suddenly they had both disappeared from view.

'No!'

Alex swore under his breath. This was an absolute disaster.

What the hell were they supposed to do now?

But he knew what he had to do. He had to organise S&R. He needed to send out a search party.

He mobilised the team—Finn, Liam, Duncan and himself—but an S&R effort was useless without a plan. Where did they start the search? There was nothing out there. Miles and miles of nothing. Gabe and the doc could be anywhere and to complicate things further, chances were high that they weren't even together. There was no way of knowing where the wind might have taken them.

He consulted with Michelle to try to work out where they might have ended up.

'The wind gust peaked at one hundred and eighty-three kilometres an hour,' Michelle said. 'They could be miles away. Your best bet is to start the search in this area,' she said, pointing to an area south-east of the station.

A decision was made to map out a grid that could then be searched in a zig-zag pattern, but it was all based on an educated guess at best. But he had no other option.

Alex sent Finn to gather medical supplies, while Liam and Duncan fetched two Hägglunds from the machinery shed. 'Make sure you clip yourselves onto the guide ropes and put a portable GPS unit in your pocket just in case,' he instructed. If Gabe and Sophie had GPS trackers on them it would make this S&R much easier, but while that had been discussed in OH&S meetings, it wasn't a policy. Not yet.

Somehow, eventually, Sophie managed to stop tumbling. She got herself onto her back and stayed there. She was hoping her clothing would protect her from the abrasive ice but she had very little time to think. Her brain shut down—she didn't want to think about what was happening.

The wind continued to push her across the ice. She had no idea how long she had been at the mercy of the wind. Seconds or minutes? There was no way of knowing.

She just hoped the wind would give up its hold on her eventually, although she had no idea what she would do then. Then, without warning, she slammed against something solid. The force was so great that the air was knocked out of her lungs but at least she was no longer being hurled across the ice. Something had blocked her path and forced the wind to let her go.

She was struggling to breathe. *Relax, relax,* she told herself, until finally she was able to take a shallow breath in and she felt her dizziness recede.

There was a flash of red as the wind carried something past her. She could only assume it was Gabe. She turned her head in time to see him smack against the same obstruction that had stopped her flight and she heard the air whoosh out of his lungs.

They had crashed against a rocky outcrop. She had been thrown against an icy slope that acted as a buffer between her and the rocks, but she could see that Gabe had come to rest against exposed rocks.

Gingerly, she tested her limbs and was relieved to find everything in working order, although she knew she would be black and blue from the force of the impact.

The wind continued to blow. Through the sleet she could just make out Gabe's red jacket. He hadn't moved. Was he still catching his breath or was he in trouble?

Sophie crawled around the rock, trying to keep as low as possible, trying to make herself as small as she could. She didn't want to give the wind another chance to grab her.

Gabe was lying very still and awkwardly. The rocks on

this side were all sharp angles, with no protective layer
of ice and snow to soften the collision. He was conscious
but she could tell by the look in his eyes that he was hurt.

'Does it hurt to breathe?' she asked.

He nodded and Sophie took some small comfort from
seeing that he could move his head without difficulty.

'Where does it hurt? In your chest?' Looking at the
sharp edges of these rocks, it was quite likely that he had
sustained major damage.

'No. Lower.' His breaths were shallow, making his
speech laboured and difficult. Each word was an effort.
It was more than just having the wind knocked out of him.
His skin was pale and she could see sweat forming on his
brow even in these conditions. She knew she was okay, battered and bruised but basically intact, but Gabe was a different story. He was injured but she didn't know how badly.

The rocks were jagged and sharp and he had been
slammed against them with considerable force. He weighed
close to ninety kilograms so he would have hit hard.

She needed to determine the nature of his injuries. 'Can
you wriggle your fingers? What about your feet?' That
he could do but when he tried to bend a knee he cried out
in pain.

'Is it your leg?'

Gabe shook his head and put his hand against the left
side of his stomach. Sophie could see a large tear in the
fabric. She slid her hand inside his jacket. She pressed
gently on his ribs and abdomen and around to his back as
far as she could reach. She heard his sharp intake of breath
as she pressed on his ribs and she could feel them grating
under her fingers. The colour drained from his face and
she prayed he didn't have a pneumothorax, but while she
suspected internal injuries she had no way of knowing. She

couldn't listen to his chest. She couldn't check for a pneumothorax. All she could do was palpate and feel his pulse.

She would have liked to have moved him behind the shelter of the rock and out of the direct path of the wind but that wasn't going to happen. Even if she was strong enough to move him she couldn't risk it and it was obvious he wasn't going to be able to move himself, but at least up against the rocks he wasn't going to be blown any further.

His jacket was ripped and the legs of her trousers were torn. She remembered Alex drumming into her that exposure to the wind could be fatal and she knew she needed to find, or build, some sort of shelter. Alex would have told her to build an ice cave but the ice was frozen solid and she had nothing but her hands to dig with. When Alex had shown her what to do they'd had a saw from the survival kit that he'd used to make ice blocks. She had nothing now.

She started scraping at the ice with her hands anyway, even though she knew it was futile. All that would achieve would be to put holes in her gloves. She had to think of another way.

She crawled around the rocks and found a couple of smaller stones. She began scraping at the ice and snow but still felt she was getting nowhere. This was ridiculous. Her eyesight was blurry, making it difficult to see what she was doing. She lifted her goggles to rub her eyes and it was then she realised she was crying. She could taste the salty tears as they ran down to her lips before freezing on her face. She had no idea what to do, she had no clue. The whole exercise felt pointless but she had to try something. Gabe was depending on her.

She was starting to sweat. She could feel perspiration running down between her breasts and she remembered Alex talking about the dangers of sweating and then cooling down in the frigid conditions. She removed her jacket and tucked it around Gabe while she kept digging and tried not to think about how the hole looked like a shallow grave. She piled up the icy snow that she excavated to form a windbreak in front of Gabe. She wasn't going to risk moving him, she just hoped a snow wall would afford enough protection.

With the windbreak finally finished, she put her jacket back on and squeezed in between the ice and Gabe. She hugged him to her, trying to keep him warm. He was shivering. His pulse was weak and thready and she knew he was in shock, and she also suspected he was bleeding internally.

'I'm here, Gabe. I've got you.'

Sophie could feel the temperature dropping. She hoped it was just because she had stopped her physical activity but when she checked her watch she saw it was four in the afternoon. The sun was starting to set and she knew that Gabe's chances would decline dramatically once the temperature fell further. She had no other way of keeping him warm.

If they weren't found soon…

She couldn't afford to think like that. She had to stay positive. She was fighting for them both.

'It'll be okay, someone will come. Alex will find us,' she said, hoping he couldn't hear the lie in her voice. Lying on this frozen, inhospitable ground, it seemed very likely that help would come too late, if at all.

She was surviving without Danny, she was stronger than she'd thought, but she didn't know if she'd survive if she lost Gabe too. He had brought her back to life, he had got her heart beating again but she wasn't sure if it would keep going without him.

And that was when she realised she had fallen hard and fast. That was when she knew she was in love with Gabe.

Was life going to be cruel to her again? Was her next chance at happiness about to be ripped away from her?

She couldn't let that happen. He would never give up and she couldn't either. Gabe made her feel stronger, more confident and more capable, and he needed her to be all those things now. She was all he had.

'Sophie?'

'I'm here.'

'Don't leave me.' His voice was becoming faint.

'I won't leave you.'

'Promise me you'll stay.'

'I promise.' There was nothing else she could say. There was nothing else she could do.

No. There was one more thing.

Unless they were found soon, he wasn't going to make it. He needed proper medical care. He needed blood. And he needed to know how she felt.

She had to tell him. She couldn't wait. She might never get another chance.

'I'm right here,' she whispered. 'I'm not going anywhere. I love you.'

She didn't care if he wanted to be alone for ever. That didn't matter. What mattered was that he knew he was loved.

He didn't respond and Sophie felt a flash of panic. Was he still breathing? She put her cheek against his nose and felt a soft puff of air. She breathed a sigh of relief. He was still alive but he'd lost consciousness. His pulse was weaker still. Had they run out of time?

She wanted to believe they would be ok but she took some comfort in the thought that if they weren't than at least they would be together until the end. She wasn't going to be alone and neither was he.

She hugged him to her as the wind continued to moan

and whistle through the rocks. It was a sad, forlorn sound but Sophie thought she could hear another noise now too, a deeper noise. Engine noise? With a sense of urgency she wriggled out of the ice break, taking care not to move Gabe. She needed to know.

She deliberately kept her back to the rocks, terrified of getting blown away again. The snow and ice were still swirling, making visibility difficult. She couldn't see further than a few metres. There was nothing but white. She listened carefully but the sound, if it had ever existed, had stopped.

It would soon be dark.

This was it.

It was over.

She was turning around to crawl back to Gabe when she caught a flash of red in the corner of her eye. She turned back, almost too scared to look in case she was imagining things, but there it was again. A glimpse of red in the ice and snow.

She waved her arms and burst into tears as two square, boxy Hägglunds emerged from the blizzard.

CHAPTER THIRTEEN

Date: April 24th
Temperature: -14°C
Hours of sunlight: 8.0

'GOOD MORNING.'

Gabe tried to open his eyes but they felt as though they had lead weights strapped to his eyelids. He was dazed and groggy but he could hear Sophie's voice.

'Soph?'

'I'm here.'

He felt her fingers wrap around his hand and give him a gentle squeeze. He tried to open his eyes again and this time he managed it but only briefly. The lights were far too bright. He felt like his eyes were burning. 'Where am I?'

'In the clinic. Do you remember what happened?'

What was the last thing he remembered? 'The storm.' The storm had blown Sophie away. He turned his head and opened his eyes. He needed to see her. 'I thought I'd lost you.'

'Alex found us.'

'Are you all right?'

'I'm fine.' She leant over the bed and kissed him on the lips. 'It's you we were worried about.'

'Me?'

She was nodding. 'We weren't sure if you were going to make it.'

'What happened?' He wriggled his fingers and toes. One finger felt thick and he glanced down and saw an oxygen monitor clamped to it and various leads and tubes hanging off him. The movement hurt his neck but his limbs appeared to be working although he ached all over. He'd obviously been caught up in the storm too but his memory was sketchy.

'I have good news and bad news,' Sophie told him. 'The first bit of good news is you're alive.'

He managed a smile. That didn't hurt too much. 'That is good news.'

'Bad news—we had to operate. Good news—the weather cleared and we managed to get Dr John off the ship. He was choppered in and we operated together. More good news—your injuries weren't as bad as I first feared. You have some busted ribs and you ruptured your spleen.'

'My spleen?' He was too groggy to recall if that was a vital organ or not.

Sophie was nodding. 'We had to remove your spleen but you can live without it.'

'Okay. I think what you're telling me is that there's more good news than bad?'

'Pretty much. It was touch and go for a while but you're going to be fine.' Her dimples flashed at him as she grinned and her green eyes were shining. He didn't think she'd ever looked more beautiful.

'Are you up to seeing Alex?' she asked. 'I know he's hovering anxiously somewhere.'

Gabe shook his head. 'In a bit. I want to talk to you first.'

'What about?'

'What happens next.'

'Next?'

His memory might be hazy but he could vaguely recall some snippets of conversation but he wasn't sure if they were real or imagined. He hoped he hadn't been dreaming but he had to know. 'You promised me you would stay. Did you mean it?'

'I would have promised you anything, I was terrified I was going to lose you.'

'But did you mean it?' he repeated.

'I did.'

He thought that was the best news of all but Sophie hadn't finished.

'But it's not possible, is it?'

'Anything is possible.' That was something he knew for certain now.

'It's time for me to go and there's no reason for me to stay. You don't need two doctors.'

'The station may not need two doctors but I need you.' He was certain of that. 'I could find you something to do. I don't want to say goodbye. I want you with me.'

Sophie stood up and started rearranging his blankets, and he wondered why she was avoiding eye contact. 'This isn't goodbye. Not for another three weeks.'

'I don't understand.'

'The *Explorer Australis* leaves tomorrow and you'll be on it.'

'I can't leave!'

'You have to. It's just a precaution but we're worried about the risk of infection now that you've got no spleen to fight it. You need to be closer to specialised medical care until you've recovered from the surgery so you're going home for winter.'

'Will I be allowed back?'

'Yes.'

'And will you still be here?'

'No,' She was shaking her head. 'I'm leaving too. So this isn't goodbye but it is the end. You'll come back but I won't. But that's okay. It's time for me to leave. You've made me whole and I'll always be grateful to you for that. I'm ready for the real world again. I'm ready to be Sophie Thompson again. This has to be the end.'

'No, it doesn't,' he argued. He was prepared to argue for as long as it took to convince her. 'It's not over. This is just the beginning.'

'The beginning of what? You don't do commitment, remember? You don't want a proper relationship. But I do. I want to be in love again.'

'And are you?'

'It will pass,' she said.

Hope flared in his chest, making him forget his aches and pains. 'I don't want it to pass. I need you. I—'

'Please, don't say anything you're going to regret later,' she interrupted. 'We both agreed this was a short-term thing. A bit of fun until it was time for me to leave. And now it's time.'

'Not yet. Please, this is important. I need you to listen to me. I know I said I was meant to be alone but I wasn't expecting to find you and I'm not going to let you go without a fight. If I've made you whole again you've done the same for me. I want a future with you, Soph. I'm in love with you. Don't you see,' he reached out and took her other hand, ignoring his muscles as they fought against every little movement, 'The way you feel about me, that's how I feel about you. I love you and I want to spend the rest of my life with you.'

'I don't think now is the time to make major decisions. Not when they contradict everything you've ever told me.

You've just suffered a major trauma, had an anaesthetic and undergone surgery, now isn't the time.'

This wasn't going at all as he'd planned. Maybe he wasn't in the best shape to be proposing but he had to tell her how he felt. She had to know. Nothing and no one had ever been as important to him.

'I know exactly what I'm saying. I want to marry you. It might seem like a major decision but it's the easiest one I've ever made. But if you're worried about my state of mind I agree to spend the next three weeks, or however long it takes, convincing you. I have never been more serious about anything in my life. Please, just tell me you'll give me that chance. I know you're happy being Sophie Thompson but I want to know if you could be happy being Sophie Sullivan? I want you to be my wife. Will you marry me?'

EPILOGUE

Date: October 28th
Temperature: -5°C
Hours of sunlight: 16.6

SOPHIE HESITATED IN the doorway of the plane as she re-membered a day a little over seven months ago when she'd stood on these same steps. She couldn't believe how dif-ferent the past seven months had been from the seven before. She couldn't believe how different she was now. Then she'd been apprehensive, excited and searching for her own identity. Now she was happy, excited and secure.

'Ready?'

She turned her head and nodded at the man standing beside her. The man who had helped her to laugh and love again. The man who loved her.

'No regrets?' Gabe asked.

'None.'

'How about all those days you wasted by making me propose three times?'

'I don't regret those at all,' she replied with a wide smile. 'I loved every single one of your proposals.'

Gabe shook his head. 'I knew you were trouble the min-ute I laid eyes on you.'

'But am I worth it?'

'Most definitely.' He grinned, pulled her in close and kissed her mouth.

Sophie kissed him back. Hard.

'I love you, Soph,' he told her when they came up for air. 'More than you can possibly imagine. You have changed my life and I cannot imagine living without you.'

'I love you too,' she said, as she looked at the man whom she'd promised to stay with for ever and always. She slipped her gloved hand into his and started down the steps to where Alex was waiting, his blond ringlets shining in the sunlight.

'Mr and Mrs Sullivan,' he greeted them with an enormous grin, 'Welcome back to Antarctica.'

'It's good to be home,' Sophie said as Alex wrapped them both in his massive embrace.

And this would be home for the next five and a half months. Home was wherever Gabe was. She'd had to come to the end of the earth to find him but he was worth every mile. She had been given a second chance and she was going to live life without regrets and make every moment count. Starting right now.

She turned to Gabe and whispered. 'Together for ever and always.'

* * * * *

MILLS & BOON®
Hardback – May 2015

ROMANCE

The Sheikh's Secret Babies	Lynne Graham
The Sins of Sebastian Rey-Defoe	Kim Lawrence
At Her Boss's Pleasure	Cathy Williams
Captive of Kadar	Trish Morey
The Marakaios Marriage	Kate Hewitt
Craving Her Enemy's Touch	Rachael Thomas
The Greek's Pregnant Bride	Michelle Smart
Greek's Last Redemption	Caitlin Crews
The Pregnancy Secret	Cara Colter
A Bride for the Runaway Groom	Scarlet Wilson
The Wedding Planner and the CEO	Alison Roberts
Bound by a Baby Bump	Ellie Darkins
Always the Midwife	Alison Roberts
Midwife's Baby Bump	Susanne Hampton
A Kiss to Melt Her Heart	Emily Forbes
Tempted by Her Italian Surgeon	Louisa George
Daring to Date Her Ex	Annie Claydon
The One Man to Heal Her	Meredith Webber
The Sheikh's Pregnancy Proposal	Fiona Brand
Minding Her Boss's Business	Janice Maynard

MILLS & BOON®
Large Print – May 2015

ROMANCE

The Secret His Mistress Carried	Lynne Graham
Nine Months to Redeem Him	Jennie Lucas
Fonseca's Fury	Abby Green
The Russian's Ultimatum	Michelle Smart
To Sin with the Tycoon	Cathy Williams
The Last Heir of Monterrato	Andie Brock
Inherited by Her Enemy	Sara Craven
Taming the French Tycoon	Rebecca Winters
His Very Convenient Bride	Sophie Pembroke
The Heir's Unexpected Return	Jackie Braun
The Prince She Never Forgot	Scarlet Wilson

HISTORICAL

Marriage Made in Money	Sophia James
Chosen by the Lieutenant	Anne Herries
Playing the Rake's Game	Bronwyn Scott
Caught in Scandal's Storm	Helen Dickson
Bride for a Knight	Margaret Moore

MEDICAL

Playing the Playboy's Sweetheart	Carol Marinelli
Unwrapping Her Italian Doc	Carol Marinelli
A Doctor by Day...	Emily Forbes
Tamed by the Renegade	Emily Forbes
A Little Christmas Magic	Alison Roberts
Christmas with the Maverick Millionaire	Scarlet Wilson

MILLS & BOON®
Hardback – June 2015

ROMANCE

The Bride Fonseca Needs	Abby Green
Sheikh's Forbidden Conquest	Chantelle Shaw
Protecting the Desert Heir	Caitlin Crews
Seduced into the Greek's World	Dani Collins
Tempted by Her Billionaire Boss	Jennifer Hayward
Married for the Prince's Convenience	Maya Blake
The Sicilian's Surprise Wife	Tara Pammi
Russian's Ruthless Demand	Michelle Conder
His Unexpected Baby Bombshell	Soraya Lane
Falling for the Bridesmaid	Sophie Pembroke
A Millionaire for Cinderella	Barbara Wallace
From Paradise...to Pregnant!	Kandy Shepherd
Midwife...to Mum!	Sue MacKay
His Best Friend's Baby	Susan Carlisle
Italian Surgeon to the Stars	Melanie Milburne
Her Greek Doctor's Proposal	Robin Gianna
New York Doc to Blushing Bride	Janice Lynn
Still Married to Her Ex!	Lucy Clark
The Sheikh's Secret Heir	Kristi Gold
Carrying A King's Child	Katherine Garbera

MILLS & BOON®
Large Print – June 2015

ROMANCE

The Redemption of Darius Sterne	Carole Mortimer
The Sultan's Harem Bride	Annie West
Playing by the Greek's Rules	Sarah Morgan
Innocent in His Diamonds	Maya Blake
To Wear His Ring Again	Chantelle Shaw
The Man to Be Reckoned With	Tara Pammi
Claimed by the Sheikh	Rachael Thomas
Her Brooding Italian Boss	Susan Meier
The Heiress's Secret Baby	Jessica Gilmore
A Pregnancy, a Party & a Proposal	Teresa Carpenter
Best Friend to Wife and Mother?	Caroline Anderson

HISTORICAL

The Lost Gentleman	Margaret McPhee
Breaking the Rake's Rules	Bronwyn Scott
Secrets Behind Locked Doors	Laura Martin
Taming His Viking Woman	Michelle Styles
The Knight's Broken Promise	Nicole Locke

MEDICAL

Midwife's Christmas Proposal	Fiona McArthur
Midwife's Mistletoe Baby	Fiona McArthur
A Baby on Her Christmas List	Louisa George
A Family This Christmas	Sue MacKay
Falling for Dr December	Susanne Hampton
Snowbound with the Surgeon	Annie Claydon

MILLS & BOON®

Why shop at millsandboon.co.uk?

Each year, thousands of romance readers find their perfect read at millsandboon.co.uk. That's because we're passionate about bringing you the very best romantic fiction. Here are some of the advantages of shopping at www.millsandboon.co.uk:

* **Get new books first**—you'll be able to buy your favourite books one month before they hit the shops

* **Get exclusive discounts**—you'll also be able to buy our specially created monthly collections, with up to 50% off the RRP

* **Find your favourite authors**—latest news, interviews and new releases for all your favourite authors and series on our website, plus ideas for what to try next

* **Join in**—once you've bought your favourite books, don't forget to register with us to rate, review and join in the discussions

Visit **www.millsandboon.co.uk**
for all this and more today!